Drunk In Love

By:

Tiece & Cole Hart

It's easy to join our mailing list!

Just send your email address by text message:

Text

TMPBOOKS

to 22828 to get started.

Chapter One

Inside the huge bedroom, Olivia was laying under the satin sheets next to her husband, Mark. He was sound asleep, but her thoughts kept her awake as her life reflected before her. She was thirty-three years old and was an independent business woman. She and Mark had been married for six years, but together for a full eight. Things had been A-1 and pretty good in their relationship, up until she'd met another brother three months prior. His name was Zay and she'd met him while out partying with her bestie.

They'd been out on a dinner date and she'd caught Zay's attention right away. Her beauty was uncanning as she stood, staring face to face with a sexy brother like himself. He admired her stance as she gazed at him with her slanted, Asian looking eyes. He couldn't help but be hypnotized by her smooth, chocolate skin glow. She stood 5'4 and her body was tight and in place like a top notch dancer. He couldn't take his eyes off of her, so finally he walked over and introduced himself.

Olivia's thoughts eased back to reality as she stared up at the ceiling. She'd found herself trying to shake the thoughts of her secret lover as she lay in bed playing possum like she was asleep. She turned over on her side, and then again on her back, still unable to shake him. Constant images replayed in her mind of the way he'd just fucked her at his penthouse two days earlier in Buckhead. Her mind was so clouded with thoughts of him until she turned on her side again, just ready to relieve some pressure.

With her back now turned to her husband's, she placed her fingers in between her legs, instantly feeling the puddle that her throbbing goods possessed. Just the thought of this man made her wet like an ocean and in her mind that had to be a bit scary. Her heart was thumping like a school girl, passing her crush in the hallway. It was unreal how Zay made her feel as she thought about his dark, lean, muscular build and his long, thick dick that stroked her walls like nobody's business. She shook her head again, trying her best to suppress those tantalizing, dirty thoughts of him.

As she lay there, her mind took her back two days prior. She remembered pulling up in the parking lot of her best friend's nail shop. It was on a Friday morning and the shop had just opened for the day. Olivia was parking her red, 2012 Cadillac that sported the chrome wheels. She got out of her whip wearing something simple, a pink and white shirt, denim Capri's, and a pair of pink and white Nike's with no socks. Her sew-in was tight and flowing just past her shoulders. The wind caused it to blow just a little as she strutted inside the nail shop.

Upon entering the double doors of the shop, the smell of strawberry's and watermelon instantly hit her nose. The sweet aroma had her feeling pretty good inside as she smiled. She pranced across the black and white linoleum tile floors to greet her bestie, Felisha. The nail shop belonged to her. Felisha was super thick, but mostly in the hips and thighs. She was a yellow bone, and cute as a button.

"Hey Boo," Olivia spoke with a smile, and then hugged her. "It smells good in here, as usual."

"Hey Boo," Felisha chirped back. "And thanks," she said, and then grabbed her best friend by the hand and immediately looked at her nails. "Girl, we have some new designs, different colors, diamonds, and everything."

"Girl, I know. I saw the pictures posted on Instagram and you know I can't wait for you to hook me up."

"Come on," Felisha said, and then pulled her by the hand, guiding Olivia to an empty nail booth. Olivia sat in the chair, and then sat her Michael Kors purse over on the table next to her. She then, reached in her purse and pulled out her cell phone. As soon as she unlocked it, a text message came through.

At the same time, Felisha had picked up the remote to the surround sound stereo and turned it on. The smooth sounds of J. Cole began to play throughout the place. Felisha couldn't help but move her body to the relaxing grooves as she sang along with the music.

"She got me up all night," she sang while snapping her fingers and gracefully grinding to the beats.

Olivia lightly bobbed her head as she smiled at the message from Kandi. Kandi was the name that she'd saved Zay's number under for safe keeping.

Good Morning.

The message read, and along with the message was a picture of him with a towel draped around his waist. His sexy abs was sculpted and his dreads were wrapped in a ball at the base of his neck. His manhood could clearly be seen as it seemed to jump out at her from thoughts of wanting it so bad.

"My God," she whispered, unable to get enough of this good looking man. She then turned her phone to Felisha's face.

Felisha immediately fanned herself upon seeing Zay's thick wood protruding behind the towel. "Damn," she said as her eyes fixated on the cell phone screen.

Olivia grinned, and then responded back quickly.

Good Morning to you, too. O'

Immediately, he responded back.

Any possible way that I can see you today?

A smile spread across Olivia's face as her eyes glanced over toward Felisha. "Girl, he just asked me if he could see me today."

5

"And, what are you gonna do?" Felisha nosily asked. Olivia shrugged her shoulders, and then she messaged him back.

I'm in Augusta. It'll take me, at the least, an hour and a half to get there. O'

As she and Felisha spoke about Zay's existence, a minute later, he was messaging her again.

You remember our favorite song?

Olivia smiled, feeling her heart flutter at just the thought of how he'd lay it down listening to that song on repeat. She cautiously messaged him back, because the feelings she had for him were indeed all too real.

Drunk In Love. O'

She looked back over at her bestie while rubbing on the corners of her lips. He had her gone, mind and all and before she could speak again, he was sending another text message.

That's right. (happy face) If you leave now, you'll be back home in time to cook your husband dinner.

Olivia looked down at her Bulova diamond watch. It was still in the early hours of the morning and if she left right then she could be there by eleven thirty at the latest. She immediately stood up, forgetting all about Felisha getting ready to do her nails.

"I'm going to Atlanta and I'll be back before it gets dark." She anxiously said.

Felisha smiled, knowing her best friend all too well. "Be careful girl, and don't do nothing that I wouldn't do." She said as Olivia grabbed her purse with a smile, a mile wide, spread across her face, and then hugged her bestie.

"We'll catch up later," she said then instantly made her exit.

By eleven twenty, Olivia was pulling her Cadillac CTS up front of a high rise building downtown in Buckhead, a luxurious neighborhood in Atlanta, GA. She quickly parked the car, and then killed the engine. She stuffed her purse under the front seat, not wanting to take it inside with her. She then stepped out of the car, bringing only her phone and her keys.

Stepping on the floor mat in front of the electronic lobby doors caused them to automatically open. Once she got inside the lobby, she became even more anxious. She headed across the marble tile floors that led her directly in front of three shiny brass elevator doors. She waited for one of the doors to open and soon as one of them did, she stepped inside it, and then pressed the number twenty-three button. The elevator doors closed then jerked lightly as it began to rise. Olivia smiled at herself in the brass mirrors surrounding her inside the elevator. Her phone began to buzz, but it went unnoticed. She was caught up with an array of seductive thoughts about Zay and the way that he loved to tease her as she anxiously awaited for the elevator doors to open. Another buzz vibrated inside her pocket, this time snapping her out of those tantalizing thoughts. She then realized that it wasn't the vibrator that Zay had used on her the prior time she was there. It was actually her cell phone alerting her of an incoming text message. She quickly dug inside her pocket and slid out her cell phone to read the unopened text message. It was from Mark, her husband.

Sorry I missed your call. How about lunch in an hour? Mark

Olivia nearly stopped breathing. She stared at the text message and couldn't believe it as tiny beads of sweat immediately formed on her forehead.

He's supposed to be working, she thought.

Her body began to nervously sway from side to side as her eyes glanced up at the floor numbers that the elevator was slowly gliding past. The wall panel above her displayed floor 13... 14... 15... Then she looked back at her iPhone and decided to send a text message back.

That's why I was calling. Now, I feel bad, because I can't make it. O'

She held her breath, taking another glance upwards at the floor numbers again. 21...22... Then he instantly responded back.

Why not, baby? (sad face) Mark

The elevator eased to a halt on floor 23... She quickly responded back to her husband since this was definitely her destination stop.

I'm in Atlanta handling some unexpected business. Plus, I'm getting a surprise for you while I'm here. So, don't ask any more questions. Just be ready by the time I make it back home. (smiley face) O'

She shook off of her jitters, hoping that her last response would hold Mark off for a while. Taking in an anxious breather, she finally stepped out of the elevator and into the Burberry Beige, carpeted corridor. She stood facing Zay's penthouse house door as her phone buzzed softly again in the palm of her hand. She quickly looked down at the reply he'd sent back.

Okay. Be careful. (smiley face) Mark

She had a split second of remorse for cheating on her faithful, sincere husband, but it was just for the moment. She rang the doorbell then smiled as the door opened and Zay was standing there. He was tall, dark, and very handsome while wearing an expensive Versace robe with the imprint of the Medusa head all over it. Standing 6'3, he looked down at her, and then pulled her inside his penthouse. She smiled at the sounds of the music playing in the background as he closed the door shut behind them.

Immediately he pinned Olivia against the wall. She didn't have time to say anything as he pulled her shirt over her head. The sight of her perky breast staring at him in a black lace, Victoria Secret bra had him on edge and ready for whatever. Hastily and in heat, she kicked off her Nike's as he unfastened her belt. He quickly maneuvered her Capri's down her succulent, smooth, chocolate thighs. As always, her black lace panties matched her bra. Without warning, Zay had gotten down on his knees, gently pulling her panties to the side. He admired her freshly waxed, pretty pussy as it spoke to him.

Olivia closed her eyes and held the back of Zay's head as her back pressed firmly up against the wall. Almost instantly, she felt the warm breath from his mouth as he began to gently suck on her clit. She looked down at him; still in denial that this nigga had her so gone. She wrapped her hands in his dreads, with one leg lifted just enough for Zay to tongue fuck the sense out of her. This was causing her to shake; her legs trembled first like they wanted to buckle underneath her. She wanted to push him away, but she didn't have the will power to. It was so good that she couldn't get enough.

"Shit," she said in a whispered tone and another moment later, she was fully naked.

Zay turned her around to face the wall like he was a police officer about to arrest her for being naughty. The palms of her hands were flat against the wall as if he was doing a strip search, but she was already naked. He had her arch her back so deep that her fat ass looked like it was in 3D, being that up-close and personal. He spread open her round mocha ass cheeks, and then licked her ass which led his anxious tongue to her swollen pussy lips.

She looked back as far as she could to see him. Her face was frowned like she wanted to cry, but it was just that good as her eyes rolled in the top of her head. She rotated her body on his tongue, letting him know that he was indeed hitting the right spot.

"I'm cumin'," she said with a faint breathe. "My God, I'm cumin'," she said again in the sexiest moan he'd ever heard.

"That's right," he chimed in. "Cum in my mouth, beautiful," he said in a muffled, deep tone.

Olivia couldn't help but to clinch the wall as she felt the hot cum exploding from her insides. Zay stood up, spun her around and smiled from the intense stare that they gave one another. He untied the silk belt on his robe, and then opened it. His goods were exposed causing a huge smile to spread across Olivia's face. He allowed the robe to fall to the floor as he stood there naked. Her eyes followed down his chiseled, muscular frame straight to his hard, thick, long wood. She couldn't resist not exploring his body as she kneeled down and wrapped her small hands around it.

"Do what you wanna to it," he spoke in a seductive tone.

The sound of the music played at the perfect volume as she smiled when hearing their song come on. The beginning of the tunes started to play in her ear as Zay pulled her up and she wrapped her arms around his neck. Zay swiftly lifted her one-hundred and forty pound, light weight body off of the floor, and then mounted her on the tip of his thick dick. He smiled at the way her mouth formed the perfect O, causing her to not know what to say from such an incredible feeling.

"I've been drinking, I've been drinking... I get filthy when that liquor get into me. I've been thinking, I've been thinking... Why can't I keep my fingers off it, baby? I want you na na." The words intensely played in the background, causing Olivia to want to ride Zay around the world and back.

Zay pushed his hard wood deep inside her and stared into her beautiful brown, slanted eyes. He turned, walking her across the wide, spacious living room floor. To his left was an all white, grand piano. He walked her over to it then sat her ass on top of it as he stood there, dick still hard while massaging the inside of her warm pussy walls. She spread her legs wide, attempting to throw it back. Zay hooked his arms under her trembling legs, and then pushed them back further. His thick, ten inch dick was slightly curved to the left as he carefully hung it inside of her, pump after heated pump.

Olivia was making all kinds of sweet moans, and then as he touched base or what one would call, the bottom of her stomach, she'd moan louder like a wounded animal.

"Damn," she whispered, attempting to ease him back a little by pushing his stomach, but he wouldn't give in. "This dick good, daddy," she'd moan with meaning as her face frowned, looking like she was about to cry again. Nothing turned him on more than seeing her sexy fuck faces. He drilled harder then plunged deeper, causing her to claw at his back for some type of relief. He had her losing her mind from feeling so good. It was intoxicating and his thrusts were even more intoxicating. Slowly, he backed out of her wet, cream filled pie, and then pushed away from her. He grabbed her by the hand, helping her down off of the piano.

"Go to the sofa," he said, ready to really get the party started.

Chapter Two

While Olivia sashayed over to the beige, leather suede sofa, Zay was walking over to the glass table to retrieve the universal remote. The first button he pushed instantly tinted the big glass windows with no blinds. After repeatedly pressing the same button on the remote control the windows began to gradually darken. The sunlight shining through previously was now looking like the night light had crept in.

Zay started back towards her, his soft dick now swinging with each step he took. A smile appeared across her face as he sat down on the sofa. Olivia gracefully crawled down off of the sofa and kneeled down in between his legs. Looking up at him seductively; she smiled, and then took his long, limp manhood in her hands. She began to softly jack his dick to the rhythm of *Drunk In Love* as it continued to beat in the background. She had both hands wrapped around it as she hummed the lyrics of the song out loud. The palms of her hands were warm to the touch, causing Zay's head to roll back until it landed on the top of the sofa. He took in a deep breath, catching a serious sensation shoot through his body. The warm juices from Olivia's mouth caressing the tip of his dick had him gone.

"Damn O'," he spoke in a whispered tone. With his free hand, he placed it on the back of her head and gently fucked her mouth. She was gagging but kept slurping on it like she was aiming to please no matter what. Zay then pressed a different button on the universal remote, causing a sixty inch projection screen to slide down out of the ceiling, a little further back from them.

Olivia glanced back at the screen as a sizzling flick played, showing two women having a threesome with a man. One woman was riding the fuck out of his dick while the other was riding the fuck out of his tongue. Olivia smiled at seeing how this man had both women on edge and trying to out-fuck the other. She gazed at the women as they leaned in toward each other and started tongue kissing while at the same time, not skipping a beat on pleasing the big dick nigga.

Watching such a sexy fuck scene had Olivia smiling from ear to ear. She stood to her feet, extremely anxious then immediately, she mounted Zay's hung pipe as he sat there. Her warm walls seemed to suck him in while she slid up and down on his throbbing dick. Zay showed her something different. He excited her to the upmost with each visit and they only seemed to get better and spontaneously crazier. Nothing turned her on more than pleasing a nigga that knew how to genuinely please her back.

Zay took in a much needed, deep breath from trying to hold it in so long to keep himself from exploding inside of her sloppy, wet pussy.

"Damn baby," he anxiously said as her muscles gripped his dick. "This is some good pussy."

Olivia began to slow grind, back and forth on his erect tool. Her creamy insides thickened the outside of his dark shaft. She knew she had him where she wanted him when he dropped the remote and firmly caressed both of her ass cheeks. While palming her ass with both of his hands, he scooted to the edge of the sofa and dug inside her, pounding deeper and deeper. He was fucking her from the bottom, admiring the way that she held her mount, but her loud moans sounding off in his ear indicated that she was about to come off of it.

"Don't run," he whispered.

"Oh my God," she screamed out from the *hurt so good* corners that Zay was smashing. It seemed that he was hitting a home run each time he dug in deeper. "Damn baby," she squealed, trying to lift herself up off of him.

"Where are you going?" He arrogantly asked. "Don't run."

"Ohhhh baby," she called out.

"No running," he spoke in her ears.

"Damn, you're driving me crazy." She called out as Zay went harder, feeling that he was about to erupt. "Why you won't cum?" She asked, knowing that he had to be close to the edge.

"It's coming," Zay replied, in between deep breathes.

Olivia swiftly came out of his firm hold and bounced up off of his dick. She didn't waste any time getting on her knees and giving him some amazing head.

"Daaaaaaamn," he let out, eyes rolling in the back of his sockets.

Zay felt himself about to let it rip as their favorite song hit its climax in the background. Not being able to take it anymore, he spit up a small load of nut in her mouth as she pulled it out to let the rest of it hit her in the face. He rubbed it in, enjoying the feel of her smooth skin against his swollen, sensitive dick head. They intimately gazed at each other then burst out laughing at the lyrics now playing from the song.

Now eat the cake, Anna Mae... Say eat the cake, Anna Mae.

Olivia took in a satisfying deep breath as Mark rolled over, wrapping his arms around her. It was nothing like being brought back to reality and very quickly. She attempted to smile in her sleep as if feeling her husband's arms around her body made her feel safe and warm. However, the only arms she wished she was in were Zay's.

Mark reached down and rubbed between her legs. She was soaking wet as if she'd squirted in her sleep. She pretended to squirm a little bit as she opened her eyes meeting up with his. He smiled.

"Damn," he chuckled, and then asked. "Wet dream?"

She put on her fake smile, knowing that he could never make her feel like her thoughts just did. "I don't know what's going on down there." She lied, still smiling in a believable manner. She'd hit the same smile on him the day she returned from Atlanta after seeing Zay. She'd bought him a couple pair of Tom Ford shoes and a shiny, new Cartier watch. She'd also gotten him a couple of new shirts out of Zay's closet since they wore the same size clothes, being nearly the same height and build. He never minded her business meetings out of town, because he got to enjoy all the goodies she'd bring back with her.

She wiped her eyes like she was trying to wake up then leaned over and kissed him. "Morning baby," she spoke.

Mark still had his fingers in the fold of her pussy lips as he smiled at her. "Good morning, baby." He spoke back. "Are you cooking breakfast?"

She casually moved his hand then rolled out of bed. "If that's what my husband wants." She grabbed her robe, putting it on. Glancing back at Mark caused her to smile. In that split second, she saw the man that she'd fallen in love with years prior. For two years they were engaged, and then they had a nice, small wedding with a few family members and friends. Now total, it was eight years later and things had really fizzled in her marriage.

"Come here," he said, watching her as she fumbled through the clothes in the drawer for something to wear for the day.

"What's up?" she asked, not wanting to look back at him, feeling a bit guilty for her indecent actions with Zay.

"Hey," he called out to get her attention. She looked back and shyly smiled. Mark was still a very handsome man. He had smooth chocolate skin and honey colored eyes that stood out as he stared at her. His dark hair was cut low, showing off his pretty, deep waves. His goatee was neatly trimmed and only accentuated his nice, pearly white smile. "I think I'd like to eat you for breakfast since I'm off today." He flirted.

"That actually sounds good." She said, watching him get out of bed and slipping his feet inside his bedroom shoes.

He walked up on her, wrapping his arms around her waist. "I just wanna eat you this morning. I can skip breakfast."

"Sounds like you wanna do something spontaneous," Olivia said, thinking that Mark didn't have a spontaneous bone in his body. He was old fashioned and even though he was packing with a nice size dick, he was unaware of how to use it properly. She stayed on the bottom since missionary was his favorite position. She couldn't remember when the last time she'd rode him or he'd hit it from the back.

"After feeling that puddle between your legs, I'm feeling real freaky." He said.

Olivia was surprised as she raised a concerned eyebrow. "Are you sure?" She questioned as he anxiously smiled with an agreeing nod of his head. Feeling horny from thinking about Zay, she quickly made her way back to the bed to lie down. She pulled her nightgown over her head, exposing her naked body. Seeing this caused Mark's manhood to almost jump out of his pajamas. She began to play in her wet pussy with her eyes closed. Mark pulled his dick out of the hole on the front of his boxer shorts. The hole in which he only pulled his dick out to pee now looked quite sexy to Olivia while he gently stroked it.

He is being spontaneous. She thought as she watched him slow jacking his dick. It grew harder and longer.

"Aaaah," he let out as Olivia cut her eyes over at him. Mark was certainly doing something that she'd never seen him do before. Looking into her slanted eyes only lured him in closer. He kneeled down beside the bed and took her right nipple in his mouth and began sucking on it.

"Mmmmm," Olivia unexpectedly moaned. Mark was definitely on his grown man shit that morning. He started finger fucking her, and then licked the juices off his fingers with a tasteful smile spread across his handsome face. "Wow," she whispered, witnessing such a daring act by her boring husband.

Mark then got up, holding his eight and a half inches of steel in his hand and got on top of his wife. Olivia softly rolled her eyes up in her head.

I knew it was too good to be true, she thought, so over the missionary position that he kept her in.

Mark slowly entered her juice box. She took in a deep breath, because it always started off so good. He began grinding inside her pussy, feeling like he already wanted to nut. His thoughts reflected on business meetings and upcoming work projects, and then it went right back to his wife's deep, hot pussy. He tried thinking about playing golf with his buddies, since that was one of his favorite hobbies, but again his thoughts went back to the slippery hole-in-one between Olivia's legs.

"Damn," he said out loud, stroking her walls so good that he couldn't contain himself. Four minutes into the fuck session, he was busting a strong nut inside her. He rolled over, next to Olivia. She didn't waste any time getting out of the bed and walking into the bathroom. He lay there chilling like he was the man as she washed her face with a cold rag just wishing that he could last, at least five minutes longer.

Fucking Mark in that manner was nothing new. He'd stepped outside of his comfort zone just enough to excite her, but then he went right back inside it. She hated this about him. She had a high sex drive and she wanted him to lay it down, but he'd disappoint her every time. She fell in love with his drive, and his ambition. The fact that he wanted to settle down and be with her was the icing on the cake. She knew that women drooled over him, but if only they knew. What she knew was that he loved her and only her, but even that was starting to not be enough.

It was never about the money, because they owned a hair salon and she and Mark had made some great investments in other businesses, one being Felisha's nail salon. Mark also owned a line of dump trucks, making damn good money off of them. So, the money wasn't an issue. However, being with a boring, insensitive man that had no impulsive sex drive was killing her softly.

Zay brought out the freak in her and she allowed him to explore every part of her body any way that he wanted to. This within itself was definitely driving her crazy. She had to maintain her thoughts and her actions. She wasn't fully happy with her husband, but she didn't want their marriage to end because of her infidelity. She had to think of a way of making it easier. Either her husband was going to step his game up or another man was creeping in to steal his position. The choice was his.

Chapter Three

Zay was alone, sitting inside of his office space at his high rise condo. The only thing that occupied him was his thoughts as he gazed unproductively at his computer screen. At the moment, he was supposed to be doing some numbers on a few clients that were in the NFL. He was a sports agent in Atlanta, thirty-one years old, intelligent and single. However, being single was starting to feel like he'd found the one, but the one was already married to another. He couldn't even focus on his work, because all he could envision was Olivia's dark, naked body standing in front of him. He couldn't get her out of his head, no matter how hard he tried.

Zay was a ladies' man and had several women that he'd lay up with, but that had recently stopped. The only time he could ever remember that happening was years back when he was in college. The woman's name was Angel and Zay had fallen quickly in love with her beauty and her comedic personality. She was down to earth and seemed to love herself some him. He was smitten with just having her around and had cut ties with all the other women that he'd toyed with.

A year after dating, Angel had him thinking about proposing. Unfortunately, one night while enjoying a private dinner by himself at *Two Urban Licks* in Atlanta, GA; he spotted his girlfriend entering the crowded restaurant with another man on her arm. When he walked over to confront her, she grabbed the man's hand tighter and without hesitation, formally introduced him to her fiancé. She played it off like she'd been his assistant and Zay felt so foolish and caught up that he simply walked out of the restaurant and never looked back. He never thought that a woman would cheat on him, but one did and was cool about it once she'd been caught up, making him realize that he was the side nigga. He was indeed broken-hearted and said that he'd never get his heart involved again unless he was certain that the woman was all his. But, now he was knowingly with another... a fully married woman.

Olivia appeared in his photographic memory again. "Damn," he whispered, thinking that he had to get it together. He drummed his fingers against the wooden desktop, and then stood up. He looked down at his comfortable attire. He was dressed in a pair of Nike nylon gym shorts. Nike ankle socks covered his feet and a gray wife beater covered his washboard abs, that he made sure was tight from daily work outs at the gym on the first floor of the building. He walked out of his office and straight into his immaculate adjoining bedroom, passing an expensive piece hanging on the wall by Andy Warhol.

Upon entering the large master bathroom, he stepped over in front of the mirror, and then turned on the faucet water. Kneeling down closer to the sink, he splashed a bit of the cold water on his face.

"What am I thinking?" he questioned himself with thoughts of needing to see Olivia. He then stripped naked and opened the glass doors to the shower. He got inside it and turned on the hot water as it beat down his back. His thoughts began to cover what he'd wear once he was out. He'd made up his mind that he was leaving Atlanta for the night. I-20 was going to take him straight to Augusta, GA where his lover was. He had to see her.

Nearly four hours later, Zay had made it to Augusta, GA and was driving down Washington Road. He was in a fairly new, maroon colored Bentley Mulsanne. He was hoping to blend in with *The Master's* traffic. People traveled from across the country just to see if Tiger Woods could make a comeback. He rode through the city limits as he scoped out the busy scene behind the dark tinted windows. His mixed CD played loudly in his ears, as a smile crept across his face. He and Olivia's favorite song started to play, causing his heart to drop.

"Damn, I need to see her," he thought. He pulled his car into the nearest shopping plaza, noticing a Japanese restaurant called Miyako, sitting off in the cut. The restaurant was located next to a package shop and on the end opposite end was a Kroger Grocery store.

I'm gonna have to try their food out one day when I have time. He thought since he loved dining in on Japanese food. He parked in an empty parking space to gather his thoughts.

"Shit, what's stopping me from eating here now and having a drink until I meet up with my girl?" He said then stepped out of his car. He was fresh and clean, wearing a dark pair of Gucci Jeans, a Gucci jersey t-shirt, along with a pair of Gucci lace up, dark leather shoes. No matter what he wore, it had to be matching in brands or he wasn't going to wear it. He sported an expensive pair of Gucci shades, blocking out the beaming sun as he made his way inside the restaurant. He immediately walked over to the bar and ordered his first drink.

While sitting there, he pulled up his twitter account on his wide screen Galaxy S4 smart phone. He had to scroll Olivia's newsfeed to see if she'd made a recent tweet. He smiled upon seeing her tweet something about thirty minutes prior. It read…

Good day twitter world. I'm just hanging out with my staff members at the Official Beauty Shop today.

Attached to her tweet was a photo and Zay wasted no time clicking on it to view it. Olivia was standing inside her hair salon with four jazzy females, each with their hair looking good, and all of them were nicely shaped as they rocked their cute attire.

Zay felt giddy just watching this gorgeous woman that he was falling for. He was impressed by her ambition and hustle, not to mention her beauty. He turned up the Remy Martin that was in his glass as an upbeat, really pretty Japanese woman walked over to take his order.

"Will you be dining in at one of our tables or will you be ordering your food to eat here?" She asked with a cute smile spread across her face.

"Nah, I won't be eating anything, but thanks," he told her while leaving her a ten dollar tip, and then he got up to leave. He exited the restaurant and got back inside of his Bentley. The engine started smoothly. The car's system immediately came on playing his and Olivia's theme song.

Cigars on ice… Cigars on ice… Beyonce sang.
The song seemed to be sinking in his pores and into his soul.

"Damn, why'd that song have to be playing our first time together?" He questioned himself. He hesitantly shook his head as he thought back at how Olivia sucked then fucked him senseless the first time they were together. And ironically, *Drunk In Love* was playing on repeat in the background the whole time. No wonder the song did something to him; it moved him in ways that had him not thinking straight. One of those ways moved him out into the busy traffic on Washington Road, trying to make his way to Olivia's hair salon. As he drove, he could see women passing by honking their horns at his expensive ride. People were staring at his car like he was from another planet. He felt like a celebrity scrolling down Washington Road.

No more than fifteen minutes later, he was pulling up in a different plaza, a more congested parking lot that was U-shaped. There were small businesses and restaurants inside the plaza on both sides of Olivia's hair salon. Her upscale salon sat right in the middle. He crept pass the building slowly, looking at the reflection of his Bentley, but mainly trying to get a look inside the shop. Olivia's car was parked on the curb in front of her shop. He knew her car and definitely knew that she was inside the building handling business. Just the thought of knowing that she was nearby, caused his heartbeat to speed up. He found an empty parking spot next to a Chrysler 300 with dark tinted windows. He swerved in beside it as his car faced the front of Olivia's salon. He switched the engine off, and then stepped out of it.

Zay didn't have anything, but his phone and keys in his hand. As he crossed over the parking lot, he put his phone up to his ear, pretending to talk to someone. He knew that it was a desperate move, but he didn't care. It was a secret between him and God. He nodded his head and moved his lips with a slight grin, playing his role to a T. Once he got to the door, he removed the phone from his ear and stepped inside the beauty salon. A small digital beep sounded off alerting everyone that someone had entered the building.

The first thing Zay spotted was a small receptionist desk directly to his right and a cute female was standing behind it with a short blond hair do, arched eyebrows and earth tone colored lipstick.

"Good afternoon. My name is Patrice. How may I help you?" she asked with a pleasant expression on her face. *Damn, I love when it's Master's week,* she thought, admiring his sexy frame, handsome face, and nice expensive ride she'd peeped him get out of.

"Hi Patrice, I need a line-up for my goatee and hair." He responded with a light smile as he scanned the place, looking for his girl.

Patrice looked him over, from head to toe. She peeped out his long dreads, and then said. "Do you also want your tips touched up on your dreads?"

Zay smiled at her. "I think I'll be alright on that." He responded then glanced down at his Gucci watch. It was twenty minutes till two. He then looked back at the receptionist who was definitely checking out his good looks and smooth swag. "How long is the wait?"

"Five minutes," she answered, and then pointed in the direction behind him. "You can have a seat over there in the waiting area or you can stand here and talk to me."

Zay smiled, but didn't want to get caught up talking to another woman while he was there to see his boo. He didn't respond, but he did shoot her a killer smile, and then he headed toward the waiting area.

"Five minutes is not too long," he said just above a whisper. He found himself watching Patrice as he sat down. She had a sexy stance, caramel complexion, and a donkey butt that fit perfectly with her small waist. Not to mention that she was really cute and had a luring smile.

These Augusta women, he thought while shaking his head.

"Hey," Patrice called out as she winked at him. "Hey handsome, you can go to station three and have a seat. She'll take you next." She pointed towards station three as Zay walked across the apricot colored tiled floors. He'd looked around the shop on his way over trying to see if he'd spot Olivia, but he didn't see her. Her car was parked out front so she had to be there, but that was the only sign of her. Once he'd made it to the empty booth seat, he immediately sat down, noticing a tall, long legged female standing there in a barber jacket zipped midway her breasts.

"Hey, how are you?" The boyish looking lady spoke, dropping the barber apron around his neck, covering the full front part of his body.

"I'm doing well and yourself?" He questioned back. Zay was a college graduate and he knew how to speak to people in a professional manner. He took another quick glance around the shop for Olivia and before the woman could continue, he stopped her. He'd thought of something just out the blue. "Can you hold on for one second?" He asked, looking down at his cell phone. He quickly sent a text message and then patiently waited for a response.

"Okay, I'm ready now." He said as the lady grabbed her clippers.

Chapter Four

Mark was behind the wheel of his 760 long body BMW and Olivia was riding on the passenger side. They were on the way back to the hair salon that they owned. Mark had taken it upon himself to take the day off so he could spend some quality time with his beautiful wife. He wanted to take her out for a nice lunch date. He'd taken her out to Olive Garden and had also brought everyone that worked at the salon take out plates. Mark had the smooth sounds of *Sade* bumping in the car's surround system and she sounded damn good.

Olivia was looking at herself in the visor mirror when her phone vibrated an incoming text message. She glanced down at her Michael Kors bag sitting on the floor between her legs, but she didn't budge to reach for her cell phone. She had a gut feeling that it was Zay and she didn't want to disrespect her husband like that to his face.

Out of the blue, he looked over at her. "Your phone is buzzing," he said, then stared straight ahead, coming to a four-way traffic stop. Olivia turned to face him for a split second, and then turned her face back to the mirror, acting like it wasn't anything major or anyone important. To make it official, she then reached down inside her purse and pulled her cell phone out. Immediately, she spotted the message envelope icon blinking at the top of her screen. She pulled the curtain down on the envelope as the message displayed that it was from Kandi. Her heart fluttered as she opened and read it.

Thought I was gonna see you today.

She didn't know what to think or what he meant by that but she definitely responded right back.

I'm with the hubby at the moment. Well, I'm actually on my way back to the shop. O'

Mark looked over at her, trying to be nosey. Out the corner of his eye, he'd noticed the light turn green, but that was about it. The car in front of him had a delayed takeoff, and because he was so caught up with what Olivia had going on; he tapped the car in front of him, causing a fender bender. Both of their necks snapped forward, but luckily they were wearing their seatbelts.

Olivia's phone flew out of her hand and landed somewhere on the floor. The bump had startled her, because Mark had never been in an accident before. She knew that it was nothing major since the airbags hadn't come out.

Mark, realizing what he'd done instantly looked over at his wife. "Are you alright, babe?"

"Uh, yeah," she hesitantly responded. "Are you okay?"

"Yeah," he told her, and then reached for the handle of the door to open it and get out. "Let me see if the driver ahead of us is alright." He stepped out of the car, looking at the other cars slowly riding by in an opposite lane. They were being nosey in hopes that everybody was okay.

The car he'd hit was a Crown Victoria with clear windows. As he made it up to the driver window, he could see the woman sitting behind the wheel holding her neck. He shook his head.

Here we go with the bullshit, he immediately thought. Mark opened her car door to check on the woman. She appeared to be in her mid-fifties with slightly aging skin and wrinkles around her eyes.

"Are you alright, ma'am?" He asked in his most sincere tone, leaning down to get closer look at her. The woman looked at Mark slowly, and then nodded her head.

"Yes, I'm okay," she responded with a shy smile at how nice he was being to her.

A burgundy and gray Chevrolet Trail Blazer pulled up next to them, a blond headed, white guy stuck his head out of the window with a concerned look on his face. "Is everybody alright?" he asked.

Mark turned to face him with an appreciative tone. "Yes, everything is good."

The woman then peeked around Mark to address the concerned man. "Thank you, everything is fine."

Inside the car, Olivia was watching from a distance as she reached on the floor in the backseat and grabbed her cell phone. Not really concerned with the fender bender, she quickly messaged Zay back while she had the chance.

Where are you? O'

Her eyes cut back up to make sure that Mark was still talking to the woman. He started coming back to the car. She quickly dropped the phone back down in her purse that was still sitting on the floor between her legs. Mark was looking through the windshield, smiling at her as he made his way back to the driver door. Olivia watched him as he was stepping back inside the car.

"What happened?" she asked.

"She's alright. I paid her for the fender bender." He strapped himself back inside of his seatbelt and since the car was still running, he pulled the gear down in drive. "I'm gonna drop you off at the shop and take the car to the BMW dealership." He stepped on the gas and made a left, turning into the plaza parking lot where the salon was at. Looking straight ahead, the first thing that they spotted, at the same time, was the Bentley Mulsanne parked across from the salon.

Olivia knew that the car belonged to Zay, but she pretended that it was nothing. On the other hand, Mark was impressed and the closer he got to the car, the more his mouth opened in awe.

"Now that's a car," he stated, and then pulled up to the curb behind Olivia's car to drop her off. "When it's *Master's* week, you never know what or who you'll see." He said.

Olivia was nervous. She had no clue that Zay would be coming to Augusta to visit, let alone show up at her salon. Her heart rate had quickened from just looking at the Bentley again.

"Yeah, you're right." She nodded her head. "And, I must agree; that is a nice car." She added, and then focused her attention back on Mark. They leaned in towards each other as they shared a kiss. "See you later, baby. I'm going to take the girl's their food."

"Okay, if I had time I'd come in and speak to everyone. I wouldn't mind meeting the guy that is driving that Bentley. I wonder if he's inside the salon." Olivia didn't respond. "Or maybe he's grabbing a quick bite to eat," he said as the congested parking lot stayed packed with people wanting to eat, shop, or get pampered.

Olivia pulled the handle on the door and pushed it open. Mark reached in the backseat and grabbed the food that was bagged up for the ladies to eat. He then stepped out of the car, holding the bag in his hand. Olivia could see Mark through the reflection of the salon's window as she anxiously made her way around the front of the car, to the driver side where he stood. She grabbed the Olive Garden bag that he was handing her.

"Thanks babe," she said again and quickly kissed his lips. Mark nodded with a slight smile at her then got back inside his car. In that moment, a feeling came over him. A man's intuition that he'd never felt before, but he didn't say a word. He just sat in the car and watched Olivia enter the salon before he pulled off to leave.

Chapter Five

When Olivia walked through the door, she pleasantly smiled at her employers. Almost instantly, she spotted Zay sitting in the barber chair to her left.

I can't believe this nigga just showed up to my shop, she thought as she passed him.

He watched her out the corner of his eye as she walked straight in the back room. Now he was wishing that he should've called first; not knowing how she felt about him showing up to her place of business like that.

In the back room, was a table made of wood, a small refrigerator, and a counter top. Olivia took in a deep breath then sat the bag down on the table. She began removing each Styrofoam tray, one by one.

Damn, that nigga is looking good, she thought with a disgusted shake of the head that she was so gone over his ass.

About five minutes later, Patrice entered the room where she was at and stood next to her. Olivia looked at her, and then looked behind her when she noticed the shadow of somebody. She turned to see who it was and was startled to see that it was Mark standing there. He had scared her to the bone as their eyes met. She couldn't understand why he'd doubled back on her, and then entered the salon after he supposed to have been gone.

"Hey boo," he said leaning toward her then kissing her softly on the forehead. "You left something." He raised his hand and handed her the Michael Kors bag that she'd forgotten in the car, on the front passenger floor. It made her even more nervous at seeing the way he let the strap of her purse roll from the tip of his fingers. It seemed like it was moving in slow motion and it rattled her thoughts like he knew something. A lump formed in her throat while reaching for the strap on her bag. Once it was in her hands, she mustered up a smile, and then kissed him softly on the lips.

"Thanks," she said. She didn't even want to walk him to the door, knowing that Zay would be out there watching them. This would only make her more nervous.

"You okay?" Mark questioned. "You seem preoccupied, because we both know that you never leave your money bag behind."

Patrice softly chuckled at his comment.

"I think the fender bender still have me a little rattled." She lied, knowing that the fender benders excuse was more about Zay being in town unexpectedly. She went inside her purse and pulled out her cell phone. "I know I'm rattled." She said, thinking that it was careless of her to leave her phone behind.

"Same thing I thought," he stated when he saw that she was holding her phone. "Are you feeling alright?" He asked, just wanting to make sure that she was good.

"I'm fine, babe," she responded.

"Wow, y'all were in a wreck?" Patrice asked.

"It wasn't nothing major," Mark responded. "Right, babe?"

"Yeah, he's right," Olivia said, just ready for Mark to leave the shop. "Now, don't you have some business to handle?"

Mark smiled, and then playfully hit her on the ass. "I do have some business to handle," he said, causing the receptionist to smile at how loving their relationship was.

"Well, go handle it." Olivia teased. "I'm good. You can go now."

"Okay," Mark said, and then kissed his beautiful wife again. "I'll see you later." He headed out of the room and walked straight thru the salon. Olivia peeked around the door to see Zay getting up from the barber seat. The women in the salon had surrounded him.

"So, Patrice said that you're the one driving that nice ass Bentley outside." One of the hairstylists said.

"Yeah, that's mine," Zay said, already used to the extra flirts and numbers that he'd get from the thirsty women that admired his ride. The hairstylist was sexy as hell though and he couldn't deny the fact that he loved the attention.

"What do you do for a living?" The hairstylist asked. "By the way, my name is Brittany."

"Girl, get outta that man's business." Patrice called out from the back room, causing everybody in the shop to laugh. She admired Zay's sexy look and handsome face as she winked at him then looked back Olivia. "A nigga that looks that good can't be from around here; if so I would've seen him by now." She said to Olivia. Zay smiled, and then directed his attention back to Brittany who couldn't keep her eyes off of him. She had juicy lips and a gap between her teeth. She was dolled up and looking good as she stood there staring at him.

Brittany then stopped Mark as he was walking from the back room. "I think somebody is giving you a run for your money, Mark." She teased, causing Mark to grin since he had a pretty cool relationship with his employers. "He's driving that bad ass Bentley Mulsanne out front."

"So, you're the one causing these ladies to blush and giggle like school girls." Mark said, reaching out for a handshake.

"I guess," Zay coolly said as he shook Mark's hand.

"Yeah, I was just telling my wife that I was digging your ride."

"Preciate that, bruh," Zay responded, now figuring that this was his lover's husband.

"Oh my God," Olivia whispered. She watched them shake hands, and then they walked outside through the front salon door. "What the hell are they doing?"

"You okay?" Patrice asked as she watched Olivia while grabbing her Styrofoam box containing her Olive Garden food to eat.

Olivia had totally forgotten that she was there. "Oh," she grinned, trying to play it off. "I'm good." She said then immediately exited the room to go inside the restroom. Her stomach was turning in knots from witnessing her husband in a full blown conversation with her lover.

The moment she entered the restroom, she locked the door behind her. All of a sudden, she nervously had to pee. She sat down on the toilet and pulled out her phone. She couldn't wait any longer as she sent Zay a text message.

What are you doing? O'

Outside in the parking lot, Mark and Zay was standing in front of Mark's BMW. "Nice car man," Zay said.

"Yeah, thanks, but I had a lil fender bender not long ago." He responded, and then looked over at the Bentley. "No, that's a nice car." He pointed.

"Oh thanks," Zay said. "I've had it a little over a year."

"Nice, nice," Mark said, feeling impressed. "Are you from around here?"

"Nah, I just stopped through from Savannah. I'm picking up my lil sister who attends Paine College here."

"Okay, thought you were in town for *The Master's*." Mark said, looking down at his watch. He felt a little rushed since he knew that he had to get to the BMW place to trade cars, because of the accident.

"I actually saw this salon in passing and decided to get a line-up and fresh shave. They did a good job."

"Well, that's my joint right there," Mark said, tilting his head toward the salon just to show that he had some business about himself, too. Zay nodded like he didn't know.

"That's what's up." Zay commented. "From now on, when I'm on this end and I need a clean tape then I'll be sure to hit up this spot."

"That's good to know." Mark said, looking back down at his watch. "My wife left her purse in my car which kinda took me off schedule, but it was good to meet you, bruh," Mark said, shaking his hand.

"Same here," Zay responded. Mark eased around to the driver side of his car and then got in as Zay held up the peace sign. As Mark was pulling out of the plaza, Zay was pulling out his cell phone. He headed across the parking lot to his Bentley and messaged Olivia back.

Sorry for being out of character. I just had to see you baby.

Patrice stepped outside, wanting to see if she could get his number. As he sat in his car, he could see her flagging him. He let the window down as he started the smooth engine.

"Hey can I have your number? I think it would nice if we got to know each other."

Zay hesitated, but his message alert went off. "Sure," he said just wanting to get her out his face. "404-555-1122."

Patrice had quickly saved the number in her phone. "Okay, I'll call you. Now le'me get back to work." She said with a smile as Zay smiled back, but he was really watching the front entrance of the salon so hard that he wasn't paying her much attention. He then glanced back at his cell phone, waiting on a response from Olivia. Two minutes went by and she still hadn't responded. The four minute mark came and went. He put the car in gear, ready to leave, but then he received a text message.

You had me nervous. O'

Zay smiled while reading it then quickly responded back.

Love will make you do some crazy things; especially when you're Drunk In Love.

She messaged back within a minute.

I want to meet you somewhere, but you've already drawn so much attention your way. O'

He messaged her back.

We can go somewhere exclusive like the Marriot, downtown.

Olivia blushed then messaged him back.

Xavier, are you serious? O'

He smiled, because Xavier was his real name. He preferred for other's to call him Zay, but when Olivia called him by his government name it made him feel special.

I'll get the room and hit you back with the room number. You just show up.

Less than a minute later, she was messaging him back.

Smdh. Your wish is my command. (smiley face) O'

An hour later, Olivia was walking through the hotel doors feeling pretty good about being able to see her boo. Zay was already anxiously waiting for her. She quickly made her way to the room and tapped lightly on the door. He greeted her with a smile and nothing on, but a robe from the hotel. Olivia stepped inside the room and closed the door shut behind her, and then hugged Zay around the neck. He couldn't resist her charm as he hungrily kissed her in the mouth.

She jumped up in his arms, wrapping her legs around his waist. As she hugged him tightly around the neck they passionately kissed. His robe came open exposing his boxer briefs underneath it. Zay carried her to the bed, his arms hooked around her thick thighs as he laid her flat on her back. She was on the edge of the bed as he looked at her, admiring her body. Her eyes always put him in a strong trance as he leaned down and kissed her again.

He removed her clothes as Olivia smiled from his gentle touch. She stared at him then back at his supersized package, eyeing him down and ready for whatever. She couldn't take it anymore and just wanted him to fuck her, please her. She was gushy wet between her legs, causing Zay to anxiously want to get inside her juicy pussy.

Olivia leaned up while licking her lips, and then hooked her fingers inside the elastic waist of his boxer briefs. She smiled while pulling them down to his knees then watching them drop to the floor. Immediately, with both hands, she grabbed his thick dick and started licking it on both sides. She licked slowly and softly, taking her time, like she was counting the number of veins she could make come out of hiding from such an arousing stimulation. She gazed up at him; sucking him into a deeper trance as her warm juices covering his wood was intertwined with the luring stare of her beautiful, slanted eyes.

"Mm," Zay moaned, just above a whisper.

This only enticed her sex drive more. Olivia shined the crown of his dick head with saliva then sucked him in so deep that he thought she was pulling his soul up out of his body.

"Damn," he moaned. He was standing on his tip toes, trying desperately hard to maintain himself. His stomach muscles tightened every time she'd deep throat him. With spit oozing down the sides of her fingers and jacking Zay at the same time, had him zoned the fuck out.

He tapped her lightly, toes still gripping the carpet. "Baby, its coming," he warned her.

She gazed up at him. "Let it come," she whispered between pulls and sucks.

"Ahhh shit," he moaned while holding the back of her head, now slamming his hard dick in her mouth. Olivia gagged as an anxious tear crept down her cheek. She wanted him to cum. She wanted him to bust in her mouth and release the inner freak inside her that so desperately wanted to come out and play.

"Aaaaahhhhh!!!" Zay let out a roar from having such an incredible nut. He shot off a thick load in Olivia's mouth as she gulped it down and kept sucking it. "Damn, baby," he said, still enjoying the rush that she was giving him. He gently pushed her to lie back on the bed, and then he opened her legs. He then devoured her goods, enjoying the tasty juices flowing from her fountain. "You already came?"

"I couldn't help it," she said, knowing that anytime he let her please him like that, she'd have an orgasm too.

Zay started back sucking her clit. Just feeling it swell up on his tongue had him eager to keep licking and sucking. His tongue vibrated back and forth on her clit in a high speed motion, causing her to have orgasmic convulsions. He made her feel so good, to the point that she wished she could see him every day. She was now sensitive and trying to push his head back, but he was relentless.

"What I tell you about running?" He said with authority. Olivia's pussy got wetter and wetter. Tasting her juices turned him on more and more.

"Put that big dick inside me, baby. Fuck me. Make love to me. Just hurry up and give it to me." She begged and much to her delight, he was ready to please her; however she wanted it.

Zay stood back for a moment to enjoy the view of her beautiful dark skin glow. Her fat pussy, staring at him and begging for his attention, had him slow jacking his erect manhood. He stepped up to her again, this time grabbing her legs and pushing them back as far as they'd go. Her feet were pinned to her chest. When he dropped his big dick inside her inviting pussy, she screamed out in a sensual tone.

"Daaaaaaaaaaaamn," she said from the amazing feeling she had. He had her legs trembling uncontrollably as he went deeper and deeper.

Chapter Six

Mark pulled into the driveway at their house and patiently waited for the garage doors to slide up. He'd felt rushed all day, following the fender bender. Once making it to the BMW car dealership and having to wait an hour, he was finally given a Dodge Charger to drive until his car was ready. He took in a deep breath, feeling some type of way. He couldn't put his finger on it, but something had him feeling tense.

Once the garage was fully open, he drove up in it and killed the engine. The motion sensor automatically made the garage door slide back down. Mark got out of the car, shuffling the keys from one hand to another. He opened the back car door and grabbed a grocery bag containing items that he'd just bought from Publix. He thought about having a nice, candle lit dinner to show his wife that he appreciated her. He had two big T-Bone steaks and two meaty lobster tails. He was going to pull out his apron and get down for his wife.

He walked inside the house, entering the utility room first as he disarmed the alarm system. A beep sounded off, letting him know that he'd pressed in the right code. He walked into the kitchen and sat the bags of groceries down on the granite counter top. From there, he walked down the long hallway and into their master bedroom, where he eased over to the computer and turned it on. He appeared to be cool, but the annoying instinct about his wife being up to no good had been riding his conscious.

He thought about earlier when Olivia had left her purse inside the car. He'd gotten it and downloaded an application on her phone, which would give him insight as to what she could've possibly been up to. The application was called Life 360 and it would allow him the capabilities of being able to keep track of the people in his immediate circle. She would never have a clue that he was now able to follow her and keep secret tabs on her.

Once his computer came to life, he immediately logged in and then went to the Life 360 website to track his wife's whereabouts since he'd heard that she had already left the salon. A map immediately pulled up once he'd put in the correct information and a red dot appeared to show where Olivia was located. It showed that she was at a red light and she was on the move since the red dot was inching its way across the map.

Mark took in a deep breath. He felt relieved that the red dot wasn't stopped on a location that he would've disapproved of like a hotel or an unfamiliar address. He rolled his seat over by the nightstand and picked up the cordless phone and dialed her number. The phone rang three times and then she answered.

"Hey baby," she cheerfully spoke

"Hey Boo," he spoke back. "I was calling to check on you, it's almost seven."

"Thanks babe, I'm good. The time has seemed to go by so quickly today," she responded, noticing that that the streetlights had come on and the sun had gradually disappeared.

"Where are you?" He asked, watching the screen on the computer as the little red dot indicator continued to slowly make its way down Washington Road, sometimes sitting at a standstill.

"Making my way through this slow ass traffic on Washington Road," She said, causing him to smile. "You know this *Master's* traffic is relentless."

"Tell me about it." Mark responded. "I'm not even going on that side of town until I go see Tiger Woods play on Saturday."

"I forgot you'd gotten those tickets this year. I wish I could go with you." She said, knowing that her husband was a fan of golf.

"I wish you could, too, but business is business." He said.

"It is, but I don't like neglecting my husband." Mark smiled at her comment. "Once I meet with the realtor in Atlanta and check out the building for our new salon then we can feel a little more at ease."

"I'm hoping that you'll like this one. The last three that she showed us wasn't anything that you liked."

"You didn't either." She commented. "One was too expensive, the other one didn't have enough space, and the last one was sitting two minutes down the road from the hood."

Mark thought about the last building they'd saw and laughed. "You're right, but don't you think that opening a salon right down the road from the hood will bring in lots of money? You know them hood chicks keep their hair and nails done."

Olivia laughed at his quirky comment. "Nah, I'll rather be located downtown Atlanta, not down from the hood." They laughed.

This was one of the things that Mark loved about his wife. She was a go-getter and a hard working business woman. She'd said that after running a successful, upscale salon in Augusta for three years that she would expand and open one in Atlanta. It was now three years later and she wasn't playing about what she'd said.

"Well, from the pictures that we saw, this should be the one. The location is great too. Being right in the heart of Atlanta, the salon will be surrounded by major attractions, and delicious dining. Not to mention, it's close to the Georgia Aquarium." Mark said.

"Yeah, we're gonna have to visit that place," she said, knowing that he wanted to go, but neither one of them had been before. At least that's what Mark was thinking, but she'd already gone with Zay a month prior. "I see why traffic was even more backed up than usual. Someone had a wreck." She said, putting on her signal light to get off on the next exit which was I-20 heading to Atlanta, but she was going to make another exit onto Belair Road. How she wished that she could've just kept driving all the way to Zay's crib.

"Well, be careful, baby. I'll see you when you get home. I have a surprise for you, anyway." He said, running her bath water so it would be warm and ready by the time she got home.

"Do I hear you running some bath water?" She asked with a smile spread across her face.

"Hang up," he said.

Olivia grinned. "You always do that," she said, and then hung up the phone.

Twenty minutes later, Olivia was pulling up in the driveway. She hit the garage opener and sat there watching the garage slide up, and then she drove inside it and parked by the Charger that Mark was now driving. She pulled down the visor, feeling guilty as hell for just giving up her husband's pussy.

She grabbed her purse off of the passenger seat and pulled the latch on the car door to open it. She got out and took in a deep breath. All she wanted to do was wash and lay down. As she walked into the house, passing through the utility room, she headed straight for the kitchen.

"I can smell the onions and bell peppers," she said with a satisfying smile on her face.

"I hope that you haven't eaten yet," Mark said, turning to kiss her with his blue apron tied around his waist.

"I haven't and I'm famished." She said, sitting her purse down on the granite countertop.

"Good," Mark stated. "But first, you need to relax and take a load off." He said, grabbing her by the hand and leading her down the hallway and into the bathroom.

"I knew I heard water running," she teased. Mark had prepared her a Jacuzzi full of warm water and had rose petals sprinkled on top of the bubbles. "You're so sweet."

"I know," he said, always putting her first no matter what he had going on. "You've never known me to be any other way since we've been together. Why would I change now? You've not given me a reason to."

Olivia frowned, but quickly straightened her face up before Mark caught it. "You don't have to worry about that. I'll never give you a reason to wanna cut up."

"I was hoping you'd say that," he said like he was teasing, but he could've been dead ass serious. "I'll be in the kitchen cooking. You just relax, wash, and come out ready to grub with your husband."

"Did I see lobster tails?" She asked with a big smile spread across her face.

"Get in the bath water, please." Mark said grinning, and then left her to her privacy as he went to finish cooking.

Olivia began to take her clothes off. She threw her bra and panties in one hamper and her clothes in another. She couldn't wait to get inside the Jacuzzi. Her toes touched the warm to hot water and she took in a deep, relaxing breath while slowly sitting down in it. The bubbles covered the top of the water, causing the moment to feel much more exhilarating. She slid down further in the soothing water with thoughts totally on fucking Zay a couple of hours earlier. The man knew what she liked and he pleased her every single time they got together. She felt horny again just thinking about him. So, she put her hands between her legs in hopes of relieving the pressure since Mark wasn't going to do it.

Mark stood over the stove preparing the steaks. He'd already chopped up the onions and bell peppers and was now covering the sizzling steaks with it. He sprinkled a little more steak seasoning on top of it and put the lid on the skillet. They shouldn't take long to cook. He then popped the cork on a simple bottle of red wine and poured Olivia some in a glass then himself. He sipped from the wine glass as he heard a buzz coming from Olivia's purse. That gut feeling came over him again.

Not wasting any time, he reached inside her purse and pulled out her cell phone. Luckily, they didn't believe in locking their phones for the simple fact it would prove that they were hiding something. He instantly opened the envelope showing on the home screen of the phone.

Hope you made it home safely.

Mark frowned. The text message didn't have a signature; however it was saved under Kandi. "Who the hell is Kandi?" he questioned while heading down the hallway and straight into the master bathroom. "Olivia," he called out. Olivia's eyes widened as she dried off with the towel. The only time he'd call her Olivia was if something wasn't right. "You got a text from somebody name Kandi saying that she hopes you make it home safely. Who is Kandi?"

"Mark, are you kidding me right now? Are you snooping through my things?" She asked feeling nervous, but she wasn't going to show it.

"Just answer the question," Mark demanded. Olivia jumped from the tone in his voice. Who was this guy?

"If you must know, Kandi is the woman that I'm hiring to run the salon in Atlanta."

"You didn't tell me that you'd found a manager already."

"Can I ever surprise you without you being hot on my heels? She and I had drinks at TGIF, discussing a little business."

Mark felt a little foolish. "Oh I see," he said. "Okay, well I'm sure I'll meet her soon." Olivia looked at him side-eyed. "I'm just saying, since she's going to be working at the salon."

"Stay outta my phone," Olivia said, snatching the phone from Mark like she wanted him to know that he was violating.

"Come here," Mark said, grabbing her by the hand and pulling her to him. The towel partly wrapped around her body fell to the tile floor. Olivia took in a deep breath as Mark intensely stared in her eyes. "I love you. You know that, right?"

"I know," she said, feeling a little at ease now. She wrapped her arms around his waist in hopes of clearing any tension that had been stirred up. "Baby," she said, feeling down in the small of his back.

Once he realized that she had touched his glock, he decided to just straight up ask her. That eerie gut feeling was eating at him.

"Are you cheating on me?" Olivia's eyes stretched as she hugged him. Her lips were partly open from the shock of him asking such a question. "And don't lie." He added.

Chapter Seven

A week had passed as Olivia shopped in Dillard's with her best friend, Felisha. Felisha had to shop in the plus sizes, because nothing in a slim or regular size could hold the ass she carried around. Her clothes weren't cheap and she dressed nice as hell, always keeping up with the styles. She was very confident and would always say that she was blessed to be beautifully thick. She had thick, solid thighs, a lil pooch stomach, and big perky breast. She looked like a modern day Jordon Sparks before the weight loss.

"O', Felisha called out for the third time.

Olivia snapped out of her thoughts. "Uh, yeah," she answered with a light shake of the head.

"What are you so lost in thought about? I'm tryna ask you if you like this shirt and your ass ain't paying me no attention."

Olivia looked at the shirt that Felisha was holding up. "Yeah, that shirt is cute."

"Okay," she said, looking back at the shirt for her own second opinion. "I think I'm going to get it." She said, and then noticed that Olivia was zoned out again. "O', what's the deal with you today?"

"I still can't get over Mark questioning me about cheating on him." She said, never seeing that side of him. She didn't know how he'd even come to that conclusion, because she always told him where she was at, even if she wasn't really where she'd say she was at.

"I don't know, either. I can't get over you saying that he had a gun." Felisha said, still browsing through the rack of clothes.

"He did and I think that he meant for me to know that he had one."

"Wow, that's crazy. Mark is the nice guy. It just doesn't seem like he'd try you like that."

"Well, he did." Olivia sarcastically said. "I haven't even seen or spoke with Zay all week. You know I gotta be fucked up. After that shit happened, I called him from off the house phone and told him to not hit me up on my cell phone period. I told him that I was under siege." Felisha laughed at her silly friend. "Girl, I'm so serious. I even asked the nigga if he'd get his number changed, because I knew that Mark had it."

Felisha frowned as she looked over at Olivia. "And what did he say about changing his number?"

"He told me to chill out and calm down."

"So, he wasn't going to do that, huh?" Felisha joked with a grin.

"Nah," Olivia laughed. "But, he said that he doesn't answer calls that aren't programmed, anyway."

"Well, you should feel better then."

"But, I don't. I can't feel better with feelings that my husband could be on to me. Girl, I've been super good this week. I've even fucked him in that boring ass missionary style for five minutes, three times this week; just to keep his thoughts from wandering."

"You gotta do what you gotta do," Felisha said, shaking her head. "Mark is just too sexy to be that bad in bed."

"Tell me about it," Olivia said as they laughed. *Drunk In Love* began to play on the surround system in the store, causing Olivia to smile.

"Don't start that shit," Felisha blatantly said, knowing all about that being her and Zay's favorite song.

"I miss that man," she said. "And I know that he's feeling some type of way. I've not gone this long without seeing him since we started creeping."

"I don't know whether to say that's good or bad," Felisha said with a half smirk on her face.

"I gotta see him soon. Thank God for having to meet our realtor in Atlanta on Saturday, because I'm gonna make it my business to go see my boo."

"Your boo?" Felisha questioned. "I know y'all are crazy about that damn song, but do you truly think that you are drunk in love or just drunk over the sex?"

"I can't lie, the sex got me gone." She confessed with a shy smile.

"Shit, maybe you needed this break from him. I know you don't want to lose your marriage over this nigga."

"Sometimes, I don't care." Olivia said. "Mark doesn't do anything. He's honestly boring as hell in the bedroom. The only reason why I'm still there is because he's about his business, he treats me with the upmost respect and he's very easy on the eye. Other than that, I'd haul ass to go be with Zay."

"Mark can't possibly be that bad. You've been singing this sad song for a couple of years now."

"I know, but that's because it's the truth."

"Girl, that man is good to you and that's more than what I can say for some of these men." She said.

"You're right," Olivia agreed. "He's just lacking the thrill in bed and I guess that's just the person he is. He did, however, have a drink with me the other night, though. As a matter of fact, it was the same night that he cooked the steak for me then fronted me about cheating."

"Oh, so he drinks now?" Felisha asked, turning her lips down with a sad face expression as if that was quite shocking since Mark wasn't known to drink or smoke.

"Yeah, surprised me, too," Olivia said, following Felisha to the counter to pay for her things. Olivia looked down at her ringing cell phone. "Speak of the devil," she said, causing Felisha to laugh.

"That must be him?" she asked.

"Yep," Olivia responded, holding up one finger as she answered her cell phone. "What's up, baby?"

"Hey babe," he spoke. "What you doing?"

"Out shopping with Felisha," she responded.

"Oh okay," he paused. "I was just calling to tell you that I'm not gonna go to *The Master's* on Saturday. I'll rather ride with you to Atlanta to see the building."

Olivia took in a deep breath. *What is he doing?* She quickly thought.

"Babe, you don't have to miss out on seeing your favorite golf players just to ride with me." She said as Felisha looked back at her, and then shook her head. "Plus, Felisha wanted to go and I told her that you had an extra ticket that no one has claimed yet." She tapped Felisha on the shoulder. "Ain't that right, Felisha?"

Felisha rolled her eyes up in her head. "Mark, I'd love to go to *The Master's* with you. Plus, I wanna see if Tiger Woods would come back home with me." She teased, causing Mark to laugh in the phone.

"See," Olivia said with a playful laugh that Felisha would come through for her at the drop of a dime.

Mark paused for a moment, but the truth was that he was quite used to Felisha being around. Hell, she was around before he came around. Plus, this gave him a chance to still see his favorite golf players in person. "Okay, well tell her that she'll be my date." He said.

"Sure will," Olivia responded, feeling once again relieved that she'd pulled off being able to make a trip to Atlanta alone. She and Mark spoke for a few more minutes as they'd made their way out to Felisha's Range Rover. They got inside as Felisha started the engine. "Well babe," Olivia said, feeling anxious to hang up the phone. "We'll talk when I make it home."

"Okay and y'all be careful," Mark said, and then the call ended.

Olivia looked over at Felisha as she pulled out into the busy Wheeler Road traffic. "Can you believe that he actually wanted to cancel seeing golf to ride with me?"

"Nah, that's crazy. Mark has never acted this paranoid."

"That's the thing. He doesn't act paranoid, he's just acting like he wants to be more aware of what I'm doing."

"Girl, please," Felisha said. "Maybe you need to just chill out for real for a while. Give him time to put those crazy thoughts to rest."

"I don't even know where he could've gotten them from." Olivia said, still feeling puzzled by that. "Le'me use your phone." She said, reaching in Felisha's purse and pulling out her iPhone. She quickly called Zay. "Damn, I hate having to use your phone to do my dirty work."

"No you don't." Felisha teased. "I know you hate that I'm just making it back in town." She said, having been gone for the past three days to visit her sister in Savannah that had just had a baby.

"You know me very well," Olivia said as Zay's phone rang and rang, and then when she was about to hang up, he answered.

"I thought you don't answer calls that aren't programmed?" she quickly asked.

He smiled at just hearing her voice. "I don't." He said. "But, I had a feeling that it was you."

She blushed. "We have a connection like that, huh?" She asked with a smile on her face.

"Must do," he said.

"There are no other strange numbers calling your phone, right?"

"Nope, not one that I hadn't had saved in my contacts." He responded.

"Okay, good." She said, letting out a sigh of relief.

"Am I going to see you Saturday?" Zay asked.

"Yep, that's why I'm calling. I miss you."

"I miss you too," he responded. "I've felt lost without hearing your voice."

"Don't feel bad, baby. I've felt the same way." She said. "I'll still visit, but I can't stay for long because I do have to go meet with my realtor."

"You gotta show him some kind of proof now don't you?" Zay sadly responded.

"I do," Olivia said, just trying to keep it real. "I'm not gonna lie to you. I love my husband, but I also love you. It's just different, though. You gotta be me to know what I'm feeling."

Zay sat quiet for a moment. He didn't want his feelings to get caught up, but somehow they had. He loved everything about Olivia; even her honesty. "Well, I understand." He said, not wanting to linger on the phone, knowing how badly he wanted her, but couldn't have her. "I'm gonna go now."

Olivia raised a concerned eyebrow. He always waited for her to end the call first. "Well, uh… Okay," she hesitantly responded and before she knew it, he'd ended their call.

Chapter Eight

Zay sat on the edge of his King size water bed inside his expensive high rise condominium, hating the fact that he'd let himself fall for Olivia. She was indeed everything that he wanted in a woman. She was sexy, vibrant, smart, and sassy. He loved everything about her, but just in the past few days he'd noticed something different. She said that she loved him, but the minute she felt threatened by her husband it seemed her feelings had changed.

She acted like she didn't wanna be with him no more. His thoughts ran a thousand miles per hour.

Maybe it was a good thing that he'd gone to Augusta unannounced. The only way he'd know how she would react was if he tried her; and he'd certainly tried her.

He stepped inside his closet, contemplating if he wanted to go out for the night. He needed to do something that would distract his thoughts off of Olivia. She had him sprung with her good ass pussy and he didn't know how to come out of that hold she had on him. He had a few women he could toss a coin for, but they didn't thrill him like Olivia did. He started rumbling through his clothes, neatly hanging up in his big walk-in closet.

"I gotta do something tonight." He said, picking out a Barocco Chain, plain t-shirt with a pair of Barocco Jacquard Jeans by Versace. "They'll like this," he said, speaking of the women that liked riding his swag. He then leaned down and grabbed a black pair of high top Barocco sneakers.

As he stepped out of his closet, getting ready to go take a shower, his phone rang. He looked at the caller ID. "This could be a decent distraction." He said then answered the call.

"Hello."

"Hello, may I speak with Zay." The soft spoken voice said.

"This is Zay," he responded.

"I'd been waiting for you to call me, but since you hadn't I figured I'd call you. I bet you don't even know who this is, even though I've messaged you twice with no response back from you."

Zay smiled, knowing that he'd saved her number. However, she probably didn't think he did. "I know who this is." He said, causing her to blush. "This is Patrice."

"Non-other," she said with a light chuckle. "I'm surprised that you knew."

"I can't forget that lil sexy voice and cute laugh." He told her. "So, what's up?"

Patrice hesitated, but then started. "Well, I was in Buckhead with a couple of friends and thought that if you weren't doing anything that maybe we could hook up." She said, biting her fingernails like she was nervous about what he'd say.

"Well, I was just getting some clothes out to wear so I could get out later tonight."

"Maybe, I can meet you somewhere." She quickly added, then wishing she would've just hushed, not wanting to sound desperate.

Zay sat quiet for a moment with the phone up to his ear. He needed this distraction. It could've been good for him, but then again what good was it to have company if he wasn't good company. He sighed, and then took in a deep breath.

"Fuck it," he said. "Why don't you just come over to my crib? I really don't feel like getting out, anyway."

Patrice smiled from ear to ear. "I'd love too." She said. "Just text me your address and I'll be on the way."

Thirty-minutes later, Zay was putting on something comfortable to lounge around the house in. He was undecided about letting Patrice come over. She worked with Olivia and that could be playing things to close, but as long as she didn't run her mouth then he figured he should be good.

Once he was comfortable, he sat down on the sofa and turned on the big screen TV with the Universal remote control. He was relaxed in a pair of cotton pajama pants and a white Hanes t-shirt. He had on a pair of white socks and an expensive Gucci watch.

He picked up the phone.

"Maybe, I should text her and tell her that it's not a good time." He started the text message then paused for a moment. "That's rude, I'll just call her." He dialed her number just as the doorbell rang. He rushed over to the door thinking that it could've been the Chinese takeout that he'd ordered, but when he opened it, Patrice was standing there.

She had her phone up to her ear, as she'd connected their call. "So, you changed your mind?" She spoke in the phone while standing directly in front of Zay with a big pretty smile on her face.

Zay smiled, peeping out her attire as he held the phone up to his ear. She was cute in a pair of skinny leg blue jeans, a beige blouse that hugged her around the hips with a plunging neckline that showed her perfect sized breasts. Her five inch beige stiletto's extended her legs and the way she batted her eyes at him made him change his mind quickly.

"Nah, I was just calling to see if you liked Chinese food." He smiled.

"Of course I do," she said then walked in passed him, looking around his crib. "Wow, it's really nice in here." She said, having never seen a place this nice in person. Through the glass windows, she could see the bright skyline filled with stars as the full moon shown above. She'd gotten lost in thought, watching the view of the decorative city lights. It had her feeling like she was in a movie with the man of her dreams.

"Hey," Zay called out from the adjoining kitchen, snapping Patrice out of her thoughts. She looked back at him with a satisfying smile on her face. He was sexy as hell, standing behind the white granite countertop and holding up a bottle of wine. "Have some?"

"Sure," she said, not knowing what kind it was, but she was going to drink it.

"Have a seat," he said as he noticed her walking around and checking out his things. She seemed intrigued. He walked over and handed her a glass of red wine, and then he sat down on the sofa. Patrice sat down beside him.
"I'm impressed," she said. "I should've known that you had it like this, driving a Bentley and all."

Zay smiled. "Hard work pays off."

"I see," Patrice said. "I can't wait to get my status up like this."

"So were you the receptionist at that salon or do you actually do hair there?"

"I'm the receptionist, but I'd like to own a salon one day. I don't know if you seen her or not when you were there, but the owner, Olivia, makes damn good money. She and her husband own the place and since it opened three years ago, it's been booming."

"So, you've been working there for three years?" Zay asked, trying to feel her out. It was important for him to know what kind of woman he was dealing with. He didn't need a woman that that wasn't on top of her game.

"No, only a year and a half," she said. "My cousin, Felisha, and Olivia are best of friends. For a long time, Felisha worked there as the front desk receptionist and then she moved on to do nails and toes. When she started doing nails and toes, she'd gotten me the receptionist position."

Zay raised an eyebrow. "So, being the receptionist can lead to you doing other positions that pay more?" He asked like he needed her to be clearer on what she was trying to say.

"Well, let's just say that my cousin, Felisha, now has her own nail salon that just opened a few weeks ago."

Zay smiled, already knowing a little something about Felisha, having met her the first night he met Olivia. "So, she was able to do enough nails and toes to get her own shop?"

Patrice chuckled at his sense of humor. "Well, not exactly, but Olivia and her husband helped finance her to be able to open it."

"Oh, okay," Zay said. "I see now." Olivia never said anything about that, she'd just told him that her best friend was doing good for herself and had opened a new business doing nails.

"My cousin said that she'd help me to open my own business in a couple of years and I want a hair salon that has everything going on it. Drinks and all," she said then turned up the red wine. "This shit is bitter as hell."

Zay laughed. "You have to have an acquired taste for wine. What do you drink? I probably have what you want."

Patrice smiled with thoughts of having to be more reserved. The truth was that she loved drinking beer, Bud Ice beer. She was a hood chick all day long, but she looked real classy and ladylike in the streets.

"Oh no, the wine is fine," she said. "The red wine I drink is normally sweet." She lied, knowing she knew nothing about wine.

"I'll fix you another glass. I have sweet, red wine." He grinned. Just as he got up to walk back into the kitchen, the doorbell rang. "Well, that must be the Chinese food."

"Good," Patrice said. "Because I'm hungry as hell."

Two hours later, Patrice woke up next to Zay on the sofa. She grinned to herself at the two wine bottles they'd drank and the good conversation they'd had before they fell asleep. She looked over at him and smiled as he slept peacefully with his head laid back. She liked him a lot and their conversation was very enlightening. He explained his position as a NFL sports agent and spoke highly of the perks that came with it. He was funny and had her laughing about the craziest things.

He told her that one time he'd gone to meet with one of his clients and upon walking in his client's office; he was greeted by a fuck session. His client had two women bent over on the sofa and was fucking one and then the other. The client then asked him to join him if he wanted to, but Zay said that he didn't. To Patrice, that was just too funny and she liked hearing about his crazy life and the interesting things happening in it.

She pushed his dreads back out of his face and just stared at him. He was definitely a boss in his own rights and from the hard work he'd spoke of, he deserved every good thing he got. She wanted to be one of those good things.

She looked down at his private area, seeing the bulge in his pants. She'd been staring at it every chance she got. Then before she knew it, she had gotten on her knees in front of him and eased his dick out of his pajama pants. Zay was startled a bit as he woke up and looked at her.

She was too caught up, holding his thick Johnson in her hands to even know that he'd awakened. It was like she was in awe to see something so pretty and big.

"What are you doing?" Zay groggily asked as he felt her tiny hands wrapped around his dick.

She snapped out of her thoughts and looked up at him. "This," she said and immediately put her warm mouth around his dick. Zay wanted to jump up and stop her since he wasn't planning on taking things this far, but the chick had a serious head game. She had him wet and hard in no time as she sucked on him like she was sucking out of a straw. She was going in, not letting up like she wanted him to bust in her mouth, but he couldn't. There were only two women that could make him cum off of giving him head, and they were Angel and Olivia.

"Damn, baby." Patrice said, after giving Zay head for about twenty-five minutes. "Don't you wanna stick this dick in some warm, good pussy?"

Damn, she freaky, he thought. "Nah," he said then moved her out of the way. She had definitely gotten him horny, but he wasn't about to fuck her.

Patrice stood up and stripped out of her clothes. "You sure you wanna turn this down?"

"Damn," Zay spoke just above a whisper. She stood there in a lime green, lace panty and bra set. Her curves were in all the right places and this put a kool-aid smile on his face.

"Well," she said, putting her hands on the sides of her hips.

Zay didn't speak as he stood up and walked to his bedroom. Patrice stood there half naked in her stilettos as she watched him disappear down the hallway. He didn't say follow me or nothing. So, she was a bit confused.

Zay entered his bedroom and sat down on the edge of his bed. True enough, Patrice was one sexy ass woman with the cutest face and smile, but she wasn't anything out of the normal for him. He had women that were pretty as hell, ass fat as all outdoors, and sweet personalities of different types. It was nothing for a woman to throw themselves on him all the time. He fucked some and some he passed on. Patrice seemed to be no different. If she was trying to get him to notice her, she was going about it the wrong way.

He contemplated telling her to leave, but thoughts crept in about Olivia and her husband. Patrice had painted a really nice picture of them and their marriage. She spoke about wanting a husband like Mark, because he was good to his wife and Olivia always got flowers and candy at the salon. He knew about the surprise lunch and dinner dates and how Mark was the perfect man. Patrice even mentioned that Olivia would never leave him and that's the part of the conversation that stuck out the most.

He'd been whipped and whipped good. Olivia's pussy had him so tamed that he hadn't thought about sticking his dick in another broad. It had been three months and he knew that he was only fucking her. However, in those three months, he knew that she had to be still fucking her husband. He knew what he'd signed up for, but he wasn't going to be a fool for love like he was with his Angel.

He got up off of the bed, having made his decision. He went inside his dresser drawer and grabbed a condom, and then headed back up front where Patrice was probably still standing, looking clueless as ever.

"Hey," he said with a quaint smile. "Sorry 'bout that. I had to grab one of these." He said, holding up the condom.

Patrice smiled back. "I thought you'd left me hanging." She said, and then pulled her panties down around her ankles as she stepped out of them. She reached behind her back and unhooked her bra, allowing it to roll down her arms and off her wrists.

Zay walked over closer to her and reached out his hands to massage her perky breast as she stood there naked. He then wrapped his tongue around her left nipple, but stopped suddenly as he looked her directly in the eyes.

"I don't want to be in a relationship."

"Okaaaay," Patrice eagerly responded. All she wanted to do was fuck him so good that he'd change his mind.

"No, I mean it. I don't want any strings attached and I don't want you mentioning this to anybody."

Patrice frowned a bit, but caught herself and straightened up. "Uh, who would I tell about this, anyway? Don't nobody know you."

"Well, let's keep it that way." Zay said with a serious look on his face. "Let's just enjoy the moment and I promise to make it well worth the visit. I just don't want you saying anything, not to your friends, your cousins, or to the people you work with."

Patrice laughed. "You act like you're hiding something."

"I'm not, but I'm a very private man. Now, if you want to change your mind then that's fine with me. I'll give you a few dollars for coming over and entertaining me." He attempted to walk off, but Patrice grabbed him by the arm.

"No, I'll keep my mouth shut." She said, just desperate to make a move on this wealthy man in hopes that he'd look her way if he ever decided to get a woman.

She sat on the sofa and opened her legs. Zay loved a clean shaved woman as he smiled at the sight of her juicy peach. He walked over, dick in his hand and ready to use it. He put on the condom. Her back was pressed against the sofa and he grabbed her by the legs, sliding her to the edge of it. He palmed her ass, lifting it up in the air, and then plunged deep down inside her goods.

"Oh shit," she screamed out. Zay was working her out, but ten minutes in, the workout seemed to go left. Patrice's pussy started getting dry. He hated when that happened. There was nothing good about a sexy woman with a banging body, plus good head, if her pussy was dry. Her legs were once open, inviting him inside the pussy. Now, they were stiff as a board. He tried to ram his dick in, but she was trying to scoot out of his grips.

He spit on it in hopes of getting her back wet.

"I'm nervous," she said, thinking of excuses.

You didn't seem nervous a few minutes ago when you were throwing this thang on me, Zay immediately thought.

Zay started back fucking her. After having to spit on her pussy about three more times, he stopped. His dick was going limp and he just wasn't in it anymore. It was bad enough fucking dry pussy, but even worse with a condom on. Patrice just didn't know. She had to really bring it if she was trying to turn on a man that had been with an ass of women.

"Hold up," she said, getting up. "I have some lube in my purse."

"Oh nah," Zay quickly said. "It's probably just me," he lied. "I'm tired. I think you should just put on your clothes and go home. I'll hit you up later."

Patrice felt bad, but she put her clothes on. "Will we hook up again? The next time will be much better."

"Sure," Zay said. He didn't waste any time walking her to the door so she could leave.

Chapter Nine

Olivia woke up with a smile on her face. It was Saturday morning and she hadn't spoken to Zay since that prior Thursday on Felisha's phone. She was ready to go see her boy toy; the nigga she had fallen stupidly in love with.

Mark turned over in the bed beside her and kissed her on the lips. "I love you."

"You better," she said with a half smile. Being with Mark wasn't what people thought, but she'd put on the charade for years. Why stop now?

He got on top of her without notice, and then stuck his dick inside her wet, uninviting pussy. Olivia still opened her legs wide in hopes that Mark would break her back and make her not want to go to Atlanta, but he didn't. After a good five minutes of quick pumping and stopping to control himself; he was busting a nut.

"Now, that was good." He said with a smile on his face then he climbed off top of her and immediately got out of the bed.

Olivia just watched him with a disappointed shake of the head.

With a body like that, he should be ashamed of himself. She thought as he walked into the bathroom.

"Today, I'm going to *The Master's.*" He cheerfully called out. He loved golf. That was one of his favorite sports.

"I know and I have to go to Atlanta and miss out on the fun." Olivia said with a fake pout. She couldn't wait to leave his boring ass behind so she could really get the shit fucked out of her.

"I don't mind canceling and going with you," Mark said from the bathroom as he peeked his head around the door. "Felisha can find somebody to take her. I'll just give her the tickets."

"Nonsense," Olivia quickly responded. "*The Master's* only come once a year. Go with my bestie and enjoy yourselves. Now hurry up, so I can get in there. I have a long day ahead of me."

"Well, if you're trying to get in the shower then you may as well join me."

Olivia frowned, because she wanted to play in her pussy so she could cum right quick. It didn't look like that was going to happen, though. "Okaaaay," she dragged, getting out of bed. "I'm coming."

Olivia drove up I-20, heading to Atlanta. She had her car on cruise control and couldn't wait to get there so she could spend time with her man. She missed him. She missed their talks and laughs. In just three months, Zay had definitely put a smile on her face that she hadn't had in years. He was the first man that she'd stepped out with on her husband and even though she felt bad about it; she needed it.

She looked down at her phone as it rang and quickly answered it once seeing Felisha's name on the caller ID.

"What's up, Gal?" She asked in a southern twang.

"Nothing much," Felisha responded. "I'm just getting ready to head out to *The Master's* with your boring ass husband, so you say."

"Aww, thanks bestie for doing this for me," Olivia said, checking in her rearview mirror to make sure that the cop that had just cut across the median wasn't coming for her.

"The things I do for you," Felisha dryly added.

"Cheer up. You're gonna have a very good time. Mark will feed you, buy you drinks, and keep you laughing. You'll be fine. Plus, you may get to take Tiger Woods home." She teased.

"Chy Boo," Felisha said. "He don't want no woman with curves. He likes'em skinny and white." They laughed.

"You stupid," Olivia commented. "Now don't forget. Keep me updated on y'all's whereabouts and what y'all will be doing. I'm going to relax for a few hours with my boo before going to meet the realtor."

"Yeah, yeah, I hear you." Felisha said. "Now, I gotta go. Your husband is outside blowing the horn."

She smiled. "Cool, y'all have fun."

"I'll try," Felisha said, and then ended their call.

An hour and a half later, Zay opened up his front door as Olivia stood there in a trench coat pulled together. The only thing that he could see on her was a black pair of Christian Louboutin heels and what seemed to be an overnight bag.

"Damn," Zay said, looking her over. She was gorgeous, showing a pretty white smile planted across her face and her flowing weave pulled up in a hanging ponytail.

"Does that mean that you miss me?" Olivia asked, as she winked her eye at him.

He pulled her inside the door and up close to him, wrapping his arms around her waist. He kissed her softly on the neck, taking in the enticing smell of her *Dior J'Adore*. They stared in each other's eyes for a moment as he palmed her ass.

46

"Damn right, I missed you." He said, intimately kissing her. Grabbing her by the hand, he pulled her inside his immaculate home and led her through the kitchen and down the long hallway. She could tell that he'd just left the gym, because his boxer shorts showing underneath his sagging gym shorts always turned her on and especially when he didn't have on a shirt. She could see his muscles budging from his back as she continued to follow him to his lion's den.

"Where are we going?" She asked with a girlie giggle.

"To the shower," he said as they entered his bedroom.

Ding Dong...

The door bell rang.

Instantly, Zay frowned up, because he wasn't expecting any company. "Who the hell could that be?"

Olivia shook her head with a perplexed look. "I don't have a clue."

Ding Dong...

The door bell rang again.

They stared at each other for a quick moment then Olivia chimed in. "Go see who it is and I'll stay in the back and out of sight." She said, patting him lightly in the chest.

"Okay," he hesitantly stated. He headed towards the front door, still unsure of who could be visiting. "Coming," he called out. Once to the door, he peeked out the peep hole and saw a Fed Ex guy standing there with a box in his hand. Zay frowned again, but then opened the door.

"What's up, buddy? Who are you looking for?" He asked, knowing that he wasn't expecting any packages.

"Uh," the Fed Ex guy said, and then looked back down at the box to remember the name again. "Xavier--"

Zay cut in. "Yeah, that's me."

"Well, this is for you. Can you sign right here for me?" The guy asked, handing out a small clipboard with the paper that needed signing.

Zay signed the paper and took the small to medium size box inside the house with him. The outside, cursive writing on the box read...

Open me Immediately...

Zay cautiously opened the box up to find another small box with a word on it that read…

ROLEX

He smiled, seeing a note on the inside that read…

I really did miss you. O'

He felt mushy inside, admiring the stainless steel Rolex Submariner that was inside the box. He was definitely about to head in the bedroom and spank the hell out of Olivia for being such a good girl.

His phone buzzed with an incoming text message and he pulled it out of his pocket as he headed back down the hallway with a smile on his face. He saw that the text message was from Patrice. He read it…

Well, damn nigga. I've been hitting you up since yesterday and you've not hit me back yet. What's up with that? I just wanna talk and see where we stand. Miss Good P

Damn, this is the seventh message from her. He thought as his phone buzzed again with another message. Zay shook his head as he read it.

You were asking a lot of suspicious questions about my boss the other night. I hope you weren't trying to get with her since it's so important for me to keep my mouth closed. That's a lost cause if you are, so don't even think about it. Miss Good P

Man, this girl is crazy. He thought as he entered his bedroom to find Olivia standing there with her trench coat open and wearing nothing but a pink and black Dream Angel's lace bustier.

"Damn," he said, checking her out.

"You like your gift?"

"Yes," he said, standing there admiring her smooth, sexy body.

Olivia let the coat drop to the floor. "Well, let's head to the shower so I can give you the rest of it."

Zay smiled like a kid in a candy store as he made his way over to her. He kissed her around the neck, getting lost in the moment then was brought right back to reality as he thought about Patrice's text message.

That's a lost cause, played over and over in his mind as he looked Olivia straight in her eyes.

"Do you love me?" He asked her.

"Yes," she responded.

"I mean, do you really love me?" He pondered deeper.

"Yes, I do," she said, thinking where was this coming from?

"When was the last time you fucked him?" he bluntly asked.

Olivia frowned. "Huh, who?" She said, so thrown off guard.

"Him... your husband," Zay quickly responded. Olivia stood there quiet for a moment. He'd never asked her anything about her sex life with Mark unless she volunteered to tell him. "Don't lie. Please, don't lie to me." He said as she stood there speechless for a moment.

She closed her eyes for a few seconds then opened them back up. The deep breath she let out showed her anxiety as she hesitantly responded.

"This morning." She told the truth with sadness in her voice, because she knew how he was going to feel.

"This morning, huh?" He said just above a whisper. "And now you're here about to let me finish digging in it or better yet, let me finish what he couldn't."

Olivia tried to lighten the load with a light chuckle as she wrapped her hands around Zay's neck. "You know he can't do it like you." She said.

"If he can't do it like me then why are you still doing it at all with him? You claim the nigga is boring, but from what I saw at the shop, he seems like a straight up, cool ass dude who loves and respects his wife. I mean, why are you fucking around with me?" He asked out of frustration.

"Because I love fucking around with you," she spoke with sarcasm, feeling cornered. "I'm drunk in love with you."

Zay shook his head. "Are you sure about that or you just drunk in love with the dick?"

Olivia couldn't believe that Zay was acting out like this. "What is wrong with you?" she asked.

"I'm the one fucking drunk in love with you, but you're the one that's married to this good guy that you'll probably never leave no matter how I feel about you."

Olivia shook her head. "How do you figure that he's a good guy? I've only spoke about our sex life."

"I was in your place of business, remember? I saw the two dozen roses sitting on your office desk. That is your office, right? The tag on the door read, Olivia Jordan."

"Well, uh--"

"I saw how he brought your purse back to the salon after you'd left it in his car. It also seemed that he'd taken you out to lunch, since you were bringing in a bag of food from Olive Garden."

Olivia felt like she had to defend her character against her husband's now, because Zay was certainly on the attack to hurt her.

"So, you came to the shop to spy on me and my husband's relationship. Is that why you were there?" She asked, feeling some type of way now. "Apparently, you observed way too much and now you wanna use it against me and for what? I kept it real with you in saying that I was married. I told you that I was bored with him in the bedroom, but I never spoke of other details, because that wasn't your business."

"So is he good to you? Does he treat you like a woman's supposed to be treated? Has he ever made you doubt him?" he asked, feeling like if this was the case then she was definitely only with him for the sex and all the times she'd said I love you, were lies.

"What you mean?"

Zay raised his voice, feeling a little irritated. "Just answer the question. Olivia." She was a bit surprised, because she and he had never had an argument, let alone a disagreement.

"Yes, he is good to me. He does love me, and yes he spoils me with flowers, candy, bath water full of roses, and romantic dinners." She admitted, thinking about how good her husband really was to her. She started to cry. "But, that doesn't mean that I don't love you."

"No, but it certainly means that I'll never completely be able to have you or your heart." He shook his head, feeling stupid for letting himself get to this point, yet again. "My heart is in way too deep to just keep sinking deeper and deeper in this pit, knowing that you'll never be mine."

"So, what are you trying to do? Better yet, what are you telling me?" Olivia asked, wiping the endless tears that fell down her face.

"I'm saying that we need to chill. I've traveled down this road before and it's not a good feeling when it comes to a dead end."

"Baby, please don't do this." Olivia begged. Zay handed her the gift back that she'd gotten him and turned to walk in the bathroom. He couldn't look in her beautiful face any more. Her tears were much too hard to witness. "Babe," she called out. By the time she'd made it to the bathroom door, he'd lock it behind him. She knocked lightly on it once then realized that he wasn't playing. She hesitantly grabbed her things while placing the gift on his bed and before she left she spoke to him from the other side of the bathroom door...

"For the record, I do love you."

50

Chapter Ten

Olivia canceled her meeting with the realtor and headed straight back home. The two hour ride down I-20 was sickening. She didn't know what made Zay feel that way, but whatever it was had her fucked up, too. She wanted to call Felisha for some friendly advice, but Felisha was already out with Mark doing her a favor. Getting home and soaking in a Jacuzzi full of hot water and a full bottle of red wine close by was exactly what she felt like she needed.

She wanted to drown her sorrows and linger in the pain of Zay leaving her. It was a part of her that felt like the pain still being there meant that he was still close by. She didn't want to lose him and it hurt like hell that he'd just called it quits, straight like that.

She looked down at her phone, noticing that it was her mom calling. She and her mom had one of those love, hate relationships. She almost hated to answer.

"Hi mom," she answered. "Or is this Dr. Jackson, today?"

"Stop with the Dr. Jackson jokes," she said, knowing that was Olivia's way of teasing her. "And, hi to you too, O'; what are you doing?" She calmly asked as if she was the sweetest, most loving woman in the world.

"I'm heading from Atlanta." She stated.

"What was your reason for going there? What have you been up, too? Why haven't I been hearing from you as much, lately?"

"I went to Atlanta to talk with our realtor about the building space for our new salon. I've been up to the same ol' same ol', just a different day. Aaaaaand," she dragged. "You would hear from me more if you called to speak to me as my mom and not as my Financial Advisor or shall I say my Psychiatrist."

"I only try to look out for your best interest."

"So you always say." Olivia mumbled.

"Well, I'd heard from your sister that you and Mark were planning on opening a salon in Atlanta."

Olivia turned up her lip. "Funny, I told her not to mention that." She said with sarcasm, feeling like her sister would throw her under the bus quick, just so their mom would stay out of her business.

"Well, you should've told me," she said.

"Why, so you could've told me what a bad idea that would be?" Olivia asked, because her mom always wanted to be in on everything she and her sister had going on, whether it was dealing with business, their social life, or their men; she didn't discriminate.

Mrs. Jackson kept going as if to ignore her daughter. "Well, if you ask me--"

"I didn't," Olivia cut in. *I never do*, she silently thought with an irritated shake of the head.

"Well, if you ask me," Mrs. Jackson carried on. "I do think that it's a bad idea. About as bad of an idea as it was for you and Mark to invest in helping Felisha start her own business," she said.

"Mom, don't start this. I'm really not in the mood."

"You should listen to me sometimes."

"All my life, that's all I've heard from you. You're so controlling. You want us to be like you so bad."

"What's wrong with wanting your daughters to be successful Doctors? Your father and I have made a great living off of it and so have you and your sister. You didn't have to be a Psychiatrist, like us. You could've been anything like a professor or an attorney--"

"Mom please," Olivia said taking in a deep breath. She didn't see anything wrong with making a wise investment in an upscale hair salon, one that was making her and her husband some really good money.

"Come on, O'." Mrs. Jackson sincerely said. "Give me some slack here. Look, I know what I know and it has always been about business and family for me. I've been with your father for thirty-six years. I love him. He's not perfect, but he's perfect for me. I've always wanted that for you and your sister. I planned everything I am today from the moment that I was ten years old and it all happened just as I planned it, including you and your sister." She said, just wanting to get through to her daughter. "Your salon is doing well, I admit. I just think you need to keep it for a few more years before you expand to another city. You've already made a not so smart move with Felisha. See how that works out first, before adding too much on your plate too soon."

"I hear you, Dr. Jackson." Olivia nonchalantly responded.

"Look at your sister. She started out going to school to become a teacher, got a degree in that, but never pursued it. Now, she lives in Marietta and has opened an Urban Clothing store... or boutique, so she calls it."

"And she's had it over a year and it's doing good. It's in a popular location and I can see her business expanding."

"Tell me that in the next three to five years."

"See, mom. I have to go." Olivia said. She couldn't deal with the break-up of Zay, plus listen to her mom's shenanigans of not being totally proud of who her daughter's had become.

"Olivia," Mrs. Jackson called out. "Come to dinner next Sunday. I'm talking your sister into coming home next weekend for her birthday. Oh and don't be a stranger. You can call me."

"Okay mom," Olivia said and before Mrs. Jackson could say something else, she hung up.

The closer she got to her house, the sicker she started to feel. She didn't know if she was having symptoms of a broken heart, but it was a familiar feeling she'd experienced in her past. Picking back up her phone, she dialed her husband's number.

"Hey baby," he answered after a couple of rings.

"Hey babe," she spoke back.

"Is everything okay? Have you made it to the A, yet?"

"No, I'm actually closer to home now, than I am to Atlanta." She responded.

"What happened?" He asked.

"I canceled with our realtor. I just wasn't feeling well. I started getting anxiety just out the blue and it was kind of bad, and then mom called."

"My gosh," Mark dragged, already knowing how Mrs. Jackson could be. "She found out that you were opening a salon in Atlanta, didn't she?"

"Yep, and you know who told her."

"I told you not to tell Zoe, but you did, anyway."

"Yeah well, she's my sister and I tell her everything."

"You gon' learn." Mark chimed in.

Olivia ignored him. "Well, mom certainly had something to say about it. She thinks I should wait a few more years before I open another salon in another city. Plus, she is still tripping about the investment we made in Felisha's nail shop." She added.

"Don't let your mom get to you. If you want to wait on opening a shop in Atlanta then we'll wait. If you want to do it now, then we'll do it now. Just know that I'm with you, whatever you decide."

53

"I know, baby." Olivia said, feeling grateful for having a husband like Mark during times like this.

"Do you need me to come home? I know how you get with that anxiety."

"No, I'm good. I'm just gonna go home and soak in the Jacuzzi with a bottle of wine."

"Yeah, go take a breather," Mark said. "You've had a rough week with the back and forth traveling and the shop has been crazy busy because of *The Master's* week. You just need a break and you'll figure it out. You always do. Take a pill or something if you have too."

"Okay, baby. Have fun and tell Felisha that I'm on my way back, but I'll call her later. I'm just gonna take a much needed nap after I soak."

"I think that's what you need and I'll tell her," Mark said. "Call me if you need me." And with that, they ended their call.

A little less than an hour later, Olivia was walking through her front door. She was miserable already, knowing that Zay had dumped her like a bad habit. She went straight into the wine cooler and grabbed a fresh bottle of red wine. Then she headed down the hallway and straight into the master bathroom. She turned on the water inside the Jacuzzi and squirted some Lavender Chamomile bubble bath in it to soothe her aching heart and wash her stress away. She opened the medicine cabinet and took a Klonopin.

Twenty minutes later, she was soaking in the warmest, most relaxing water she'd ever felt. Each time she'd soak like this only felt better and better, but she sat in it and cried. She was feeling hurt over not knowing how to feel about her feelings for Zay. She just didn't see it coming. A part of her wanted to embrace the break-up and just make things right with Mark, but another part of her didn't want Mark anymore.

Her mother crossed her mind and this only made things worse. Sometimes, she could say the damndest things that made sense, but then sometimes she didn't. Her mom had made just living a normal life, difficult. Mrs. Jackson didn't raise any slackers and she was very hard on them in being successful and in settling down early on and establishing a strong foundation with their husbands; if they ever married.

She thought back when her mom didn't like Mark. She didn't think he was right for her. To her, he was too good to be true. But over time, he'd proven his loyalty and had even gotten Mrs. Jackson on his side fully. She loved him and treated him like her own son and because of that he didn't get any more slack than she gave her girls.

Olivia sighed, because Mark was too good to be true. His sex game was wack and it put a serious strain on her marriage. So serious, that she'd fallen drunk in love with another. After revealing to her sister once that Mark's sex game was about as awful as it came, she'd said to her back then...

O', you've been faithful to this man for a long time. Deal with it if you want your marriage to work. Don't go looking to get fucked senseless, because if that happens… Your marriage will be over.

"Damn, I should've listened to Zoe." She said out loud, drowning her sorrows with the bottle of wine in her hand as she turned it up. She cried, because she hadn't been in love with Mark for years. She didn't believe that she ever loved him. She just loved the good-hearted man that he was. It had nothing to do with seeing him and feeling her heart flutter each time, it was just his good nature, nice sense of humor, and hot body. He didn't even kiss her like it was real.

An hour and half had passed with Olivia still in the tub, soaking away her problems. Her phone rang, disturbing her thoughts and she looked over on the counter next to the Jacuzzi. She could see that it was Felisha. She dried her hands on the towel sitting nearby then answered the phone.

"Hey," she spoke like she was sad.

"You okay?" Felicia asked with concern in her voice.

"I'm good." Olivia responded, but she knew that Felisha had known better. She almost knew her better than her own sister. They'd been best of friends since pre-school, and living down the road from each other in the same prestigious neighborhood. However, when they got older, Felisha moved in a different area, a different district and this separated the girls. However, they always remained best of friends.

"You don't sound good," Felisha probed.

"Where's Mark?" Olivia quickly asked.

"He walked inside the store to pay for the gas.

Olivia took in a saddening deep breath. "He broke up with me." She informed her.

"Aww," Felisha said. "What happened?"

"I don't know. Things were going good and then he started questioning me about my marriage."

"Your marriage," Felisha said. "Why was he questioning you about your marriage?"

"I don't know. He just started asking questions and I wasn't saying what he wanted to hear. He just feels that I'll never leave Mark."

"Well," Felisha cut in with a raised eyebrow. "Will you?"

"Nope," she said then feeling unsure. "I don't know," she stated.

55

"You're talking that foolish shit now," Felisha said.

"It doesn't matter what I do. All I know is that right now, I'm not happy in my marriage."

"Oh, yeah well. I'm glad you took something for that headache and since you've taken a calmer you can get some rest now." Felisha said as Mark got back inside the car. "Your hubby said he's about to call you."

Olivia had caught on immediately once the conversation changed. "Okay, and tell Mark to fix your back porch light before he leaves. I don't like you and my nephew walking in through the back with the light off like that at night."

"Yes ma'am." Felisha said. "I'll call you later." And then they ended their call.

A few hours had passed, and Olivia was sitting on her plush, king size, rice bed watching *Scandal* that she'd set up a series recording, on her DVR. This was one of her favorite TV shows. It sort of reminded her of her life except she was the wife cheating on her husband instead of it being the other way around.

She was sad and still feeling hurt from Zay pushing her away. She couldn't believe that he'd been so cold towards her after things had been so good for three months without the craziness. She grabbed her iPhone off of the nightstand to check her Twitter account. She wanted to see if he'd logged in and said something. She scrolled through the newsfeed, but then decided to just go to his page. She frowned while reading the most current tweet that he'd posted about two hours prior.

Hanging out with my Bro, Dillon. We bout to see what's poppn' tonight.

"Oh, so he's chilling with his brother tonight," she said, trying not to think that he was out looking for some new pussy in hopes of getting over hers. "Who the hell am I fooling?" Zay hadn't attempted to text her or nothing. She was definitely sick, thinking about the women that were probably hanging in his face, wanting a piece of his sexy ass.

She sat there missing him. So, she signed into her Instagram account just to go through his sexy pictures. As she clicked from one picture to the other, her eyes suddenly widened as she clicked on a photo that had just posted to his page within seconds of her being nosey. The photo showed a pretty, video vixen looking chick, sitting in his lap at the club. To top it off, she had her painted on red lips stuck to the side of his face like he was her man. She was disgusted at what he'd had the nerve to say concerning the picture as it read ...

I've missed this.

"Is he fucking serious right now?" She asked, feeling the need to talk to somebody. She immediately called Felisha's phone, but didn't get an answer. Knowing Felisha, she probably had company over. She always had a different man. Olivia sometimes thought that she just didn't want to settle down. Maybe it was the company of different men that kept her attention off of her one true love; her no good baby daddy that was never ever around.

She quickly glanced back at his Instagram page just to get another look at the disturbing photo. It had her stomach turning in knots.

"Is this nigga testing me?" She wondered and then went to her Twitter account and started typing on the key pad of her cell phone.

Hubby is out with the guys. I can't wait until he gets home so I can rest my weary head on his loving chest.

"Let's see how that makes him feel since he's so worried about how good my husband is to me." She said, and then pressed enter as she smiled once her message showed up on her twitter newsfeed.

She lay back, not wanting to be petty, but Zay was bringing out different emotions. Emotions, she didn't realize that she had. In the past eight years of being with Mark, he'd never disrespected her. He better not had thought about ever doing her like that.

She pulled the covers up around her neck and logged off of Twitter and Instagram accounts. Zay already had gotten one reaction out of her and if he posted one more picture, he was sure to get another one. Logging off was her best bet at the moment. She didn't know how she would shake him, but one thing's for sure; it wasn't going to be easy to do.

Chapter Eleven

Zay sat at his computer desk inside of his office going over some numbers. He was already scouting players for the upcoming draft season. He looked up as he heard a tap on the door.

"What's up, Bro?" Dillon spoke.

"What's up, Bro?" Zay spoke back. "I know I gave you a key for emergency purposes, but I don't see nothing major going on 'round here," he said, looking around the room, with a wandering eye like he was looking for something.

Dillon laughed, stepping inside the office and immediately sitting down on the beige leather love seat. "I see you're stuck in your work as usual."

"That's the only way to get it." Zay said with a smile on his face. You already know how it is, Mr. Up and Coming concert promoter."

"I know right," Dillon said with a cool smile.

"So, what brings you by little brother?"

"I was just in the area, meeting one of the girls we clubbed with Saturday night."

Zay looked over at his handsome lil brother and approvingly nodded his head. "That's what's up." He coolly said.

"Yeah, she ain't nobody I can see myself chilling with, though." He commented, shaking his head.

"She lives in this building?" Zay asked, figuring that the chick must've had some money to be living where he lived. And, if his brother didn't want a female with her own then something had to be wrong with her.

"Yeah, but she ain't look nothing like she did in the club that night," he said like his stomach started hurting just thinking about it. "See, she told me that she didn't have a man and that I could stop by and surprise her. I know I was drinking heavily that night, but damn I think I would've remembered if the girl was missing a tooth."

Zay laughed out loud. "What nigga? She didn't have no tooth?"

"Check this out, Bro. I go to her crib and I ring the doorbell, right. I'm standing there waiting for her sexy ass to open the door," he said with a sneaky look on his face. "Shit, I was gonna fuck if she was down, but she opened the door, handing me a twenty dollar bill. Shit, I reached for the money. If she giving out hot dubs like that then I'm that guy." Zay grinned, because no telling what else was about to come out of Dillon's mouth. He was a straight clown. "So, when she realized who I was, right." He said with right being his favorite way to end a sentence like he was really about to make a point. "She snatched the money back then looked in my face, covering her mouth."

"What the hell?" Zay curiously pondered while laughing.

"She talking about, she thought I was the pizza man." They laughed out loud. "She tried covering up, but I saw that missing tooth right on the side of her mouth. Then on top of that, she had a wet head, from just washing her hair and it was shorter than mine." He said, rubbing across the smooth waves in his jet black, temple tape hair cut.

"Nigga you foolish," Zay continued to laugh.

"We men need to thank God every day for weave," he said with a serious look on his face. "Oh and make-up, too because she was also missing that and looking rough as hell," he chuckled. "Talking about, she didn't know I was coming four days later. She thought I would've showed up the next day." Dillon shook his head for the umpteenth time. "Hell, it was a surprise. She wasn't supposed to know."

Zay laughed so hard he could hardly catch his breath.

"Bro, she looked shame as hell. Her lil friend was over there to do her hair. I know she was wishing that I would've just come about an hour later. Damn," he said as he thought about it. "She would've fooled me again. These women will trick your ass. I started to ask her to let me feel between her legs right quick. I wanted to make sure the bitch didn't have a dick." Zay couldn't stop laughing; because Dillon's facial expression was so serious.

"Man, stop. She couldn't have been that bad."

"Shittin' me," Dillon responded with a frown on his face. "It was bad, Bro. Then when I sat down, a lil bad ass dog ran out and shitted right on the floor in front of me." Dillon shook his head. "Now, that was some nasty shit. I hauled ass after that."

Zay tried to straighten his face up, because Dillon always had him cracking up. "Man, you crazy as hell."

"I can't be with a woman that's ugly and can't, at least, train her dogs." Zay laughed again. "Man, that shit ain't funny. That shit is real." Dillon said then quickly changed the subject unto his brother after he let him laugh about two more minutes. "What's up with her homegirl; the one that was sittin' in your lap at the club that night?"

"Nothing," Zay responded. "She followed me back here, but I pretended to have a headache. I just wasn't in the mood."

"That ain't the big brother I know," Dillon said, knowing that his brother was a hot commodity that not only got lots of pussy, but had also gotten him plenty of it, too. "Is this about

Olivia?" Dillon asked, already well aware of whom she was. They'd met the first night Zay and Olivia met.

"I can't shake her ass," he sadly admitted.

"Bro, if you want to be with the woman, you can't be catching them unnecessary feelings. You already know her situation. If you can't handle that then maybe you need to leave it alone for real."

"I can handle it, but I just want her so bad. I want to be the man that's good to her and good for her. It's just that her husband has already beat me to it."

"You can have all the money in the world, but you can't compete with a woman's husband; especially if he's good to her."

"Yeah, but he ain't that good to her. She says he's slacking in bedroom. That's why I got her. Can you believe that I'm the second man that she's ever slept with?"

"She lying," Dillon cut in. "How old is she?"

"She's thirty-three years old."

"Trust me, Bro. She's lying. She just hate to admit that she has met another man that's giving her husband a run for his money. They always try to make up excuses."

"I believe her, though." Zay said. "It had something to do with the strict way that she was raised and how her parent's held her up on this pedestal, making her stick to certain vows."

"That's unbelievable, man. I'm trying to tell you." Dillon laughed.

"Okay," Zay said not following his brother up.

"You serious aren't you?" Dillon asked, noticing that Zay wasn't laughing or even trying to cut a smile. He'd been with enough women to know better.

"I am serious. I mean she be so hot for me. Her husband ain't beatin' that thang right and she can't get enough. I know when a woman is experienced and I know when one is not. I lured the freak out of her, even though it was just waiting to come out. She talks about her and the husband being together for eight years and in eight years he has only beat it doggy style five times."

"Get the fuck outta here," Dillon disappointedly said. "Shit, a woman that fine I'll have that lil ass up in the air and beatin' the hell out of it."

Zay nodded his head with an approving smile as he thought about fucking her up against the wall and relentlessly eating her good pussy.

"No wonder that pussy so good to you." Dillon teased.

"You should hit her up. Fuck it, just do it."

"I've already ignored a few of her texts and a couple of her phone calls."

"I don't know why you're acting hard. You look softer than a rabbit, if you ask me." Dillon teased, but was very serious.

"Ain't nobody asking you," Zay stated with a light chuckle as a text message came through to his phone. He looked down at it and shook his head. "I got a stalker."

"Who? Don't tell me it's the dry pussy bitch from last week."

"The girl is relentless, Bro. She keep hittn' me up and I keep ignoring her. I should've never stuck my dick in that broad."

"What does the message say?" Dillon nosily asked.

Zay looked at his cell phone and read the message out loud.

Hey, this is my last time reaching out to you. I don't know what I did, but I'm sorry. Call me if you ever need company again. Ms. Good P

"Yeah, she sounds thirsty as fuck." Dillon said.

"She is," Zay commented.

"Did she sign her name with Ms. Good P? It needs to be Ms. Dry P."

Zay laughed.

"Look, I'm outta here, Bro." Dillon said, standing up and stretching. "It's Wednesday. I gotta hit the gym."

"A'ight Bro," Zay stood up and gave his brother dap.

"I think you should call your girl though. Just see what she's up too. You need to do something, sittin' round here looking like a sick puppy."

"Get outta my house, nigga." Zay stated with a chuckle.

The minute his brother was out of sight, he went straight back to his computer and sat down behind the desk. He pulled up his Twitter account. He wanted to see if Olivia had said anything since she'd tweeted about needing to lie on her husband's chest that night while he was clubbing. A part of him wanted to think that maybe she did it, because of the picture that he'd put on

Instagram page of the woman sitting in his lap. Then again, he didn't know what to think about it. It definitely pissed him off, though and that's why he didn't bother to answer her calls when she'd called him or respond to any of her text messages.

Once his account was pulled up, he quickly went straight to her page. A picture was posted about an hour prior showing her with Felisha and Felisha's four year old son, kissing Olivia on the cheek. It made him smile as he read...

I'm having a late lunch with two of my favorite people. I just love this lil guy.
#MyNephewAndMyBestie

He sat there, contemplating his next move.

Chapter Twelve

. Olivia sat inside of Logan's Roadhouse, eating a late lunch with Felisha and lil Romeo. She was still down in the dumps, but it was hump day and things were looking a little better. *The Master's* was gone and so was the crazy traffic. All she wanted to do was have a nice outing with her bestie and her cute nephew.

"I love your hair like that," she complimented Felisha who was rocking the long box braids that *Janet Jackson* wore in *Poetic Justice*.

"Thanks," Felisha responded, taking a sip from her Road House ice tea. "I love it, too."

"It definitely fits your cute face," Olivia said with a smile. "Patrice does hair good. She needs to get in one of those booths and get her ass from behind that receptionist desk."

"I try to tell her that. One day, she'll listen." Felisha said. "Anyway, how have you been? You look better than you did when I saw you on Monday."

"I'm good," Olivia responded. "I've just been taking things day by day."

"Have you called or spoken to Zay, yet?"

"Nope," she sadly responded. "He won't answer or text back."

"Well, it seems that this fallout is pretty serious." Felisha said then bit off of her Logan's buttery bread. "But, then again, I doubt it."

"I just don't understand what brought all of this on. I mean, we were doing so good. Next thing I know, Mark is tripping just out the blue and that caused me to back off from Zay, but only for a few days. He shouldn't have been tripping like that. He knows my situation."

"He's pussy whipped," Felisha laughed.

"I can't tell or he would've been in between these legs Saturday when I was there."

"Don't worry," Felisha said. "He'll call you."

"I don't know why I'm so drunk in love with this man. I got it so bad that I can hardly stand myself."

"For starters, he was the first real man that gave you what you needed in the bedroom. You weren't ready for the shit that he put on your ass."

"You're more than likely right. I mean, I knew nothing about letting a man bust on my face, let alone in my mouth."

Felisha acted as if she was gagging. "Not in front of the little one," they laughed.

"The nigga fuck me like he means it. When he goes in, he goes in." She said, thinking back at how he'd make her cum over and over again.

Felisha shook her head. "Poor baby," she said. "Your mama got you fucked up. If you would've been fucking at an earlier age instead of waiting until you got married at the age of twenty-seven. I mean, who waits that long nowadays, anyway?"

"You know my parents were strict on us keeping our virginity until we got married. Plus, I had all the intentions of giving it up way before then had Sly not stood me up at the altar."

"Can you blame the man? You'd been dating him since high school and wouldn't even let him taste the chocolate inside the damn cookie. He wanted chocolate chip cookies and you were just giving him water. You couldn't even give the nigga no milk. "

"Now you wanna trip about it." Olivia said with a slight smirk on her face.

"You know that I ain't lying. That man held out for you for what... six, seven years. I mean, damn... I'm surprised the blue balls didn't kill him." She grinned, but they both knew that Sly's fine ass didn't ever have blue balls. He was fucking any and everybody except his own woman.

"Don't act like I didn't try to give him some."

"When?" Felisha laughed. "Oh, you're talking about two days before your wedding; when he couldn't even get it in."

"I see we got jokes today." Olivia dryly stated. It was kind of funny, but she wasn't in the laughing mood.

"That man didn't know if the pussy would be good enough to marry you. That's why he didn't show up the day of your wedding," she coldly stated. "Plus, your mama stayed in your business. Just as she still do. Bless Mark's heart for still being there."

"Well, aren't we being real candid today." Olivia said, starting to feel offended. "I guess that's why I ended up with the good guy and we've done quite well for ourselves without the help of others."

Felisha felt cut like Olivia was now politely stabbing back at her.

"Matter of fact, I'm gonna do as my mom said and be good to my husband. Fuck Zay. I don't want any more parts of him. I'm gonna smother Mark with the right attention. I'm gonna give him head even if he doesn't want it. I'm gonna bring out the freak in him just like Zay did with me."

"Do you think that's gonna save your marriage?" Felisha asked. "When you fucked Zay, your marriage was over."

"Are you kidding me right now? I didn't know that my marriage was on the rocks." Olivia frowned at Felisha's smart mouth, and then she conceitedly grinned. "Wow and this coming from someone who has never been married, ever or engaged, for that matter. The same person that is called *Ms. Reliable* by most of the men that she fucks with," she said. "I'm glad that I've never met half of them personally, because I wouldn't be able to keep up. You talk about my strict parent's, but they saved me from a lot of the shit that you've gone through with men. I mean, your son's father doesn't even show up to see him, not even on his birthday or Christmas. I'm your best friend and I've never even met the guy."

Felisha seemed hurt. "So, you think you're better than me? I knew that your true colors would someday show."

Olivia was stunned that their wonderful day had gone sour very quickly. "I've never thought that I was better than you. Where is this talk coming from?"

"I knew it," Felisha said.

"You knew what?"

Felisha grabbed lil Romeo up out of the booth, and then she snatched up her purse. "Guess I'm glad that I drove here," she said. "And for the record, I would've been married by now, but you're right. I've made some really wrong decisions in my life. Maybe, it's time that I change that." She said, grabbing lil Romeo by the hand. "Tell Auntie, bye."

"Bye boo," Olivia said, leaning down and kissing him on the lips. She couldn't believe that her bestie had just walked out on her. The minute the waitress walked over, she ordered her second top shelf Roadhouse ice tea. She just wanted to get tipsy and forget all the crazy shit that had been going on in her life. She was going to leave there and go home to an empty house since Mark was out of town for the night, handling some last minute business on a new project that he'd been working on. Maybe this would give her time to get prepared to show him how it'd be to have a very attentive wife in his life.

Olivia had made it home and already in her silk night gown as she sat on the edge of the bed and removed her night slippers then climbed under the cover. Mark was out of town for the night, but they'd had a nice conversation on Tango's video chat before they decided to call it night. Mark even flashed her his dick in playing around, because she asked him to. That was something he would've never done had she not asked.

Closed mouths don't get fed, she thought. She did love her handsome husband and if she could make it work with him she was certainly going to try.

Getting over Zay had proven easier said than done. It had been four days since their last encounter and it still made her sick just to think that he was getting cozy with the next. She would be alright if she stayed off of his Twitter and Instagram page being nosey, but she couldn't get his sexy pictures off of her mind. She'd even started checking out his Facebook page and she didn't really even care about Facebook that much.

With her Galaxy Tablet already in bed with her, she instantly signed in to Twitter. She had to see what he'd been up too or at least get a good night kiss, pretending that his pictures was him in person. She smiled as soon as her account pulled up and her message indicator showed that she had one new message. She hurriedly clicked on it to see that it was from Zay. Her heart fell in her stomach as the butterflies started happily dancing.

The message was from two hours prior. She grew anxious as she quickly read the message...

Hey Boo, I've missed you. I just wanted to say Hi and I hope you're doing well.

"Damn, I hope he's still up," she said looking at the time displaying 12:38a.m. "Fuck it."

Hey, I've missed you too. I'm good. Hope you're doing well also.

A few minutes passed and as Olivia had gotten in her mind that Zay was probably asleep or just not responding again, a message popped up on her screen. She was ecstatic as she quickly opened it up and read it.

Damn, I was just thinking about you.

She blushed then responded.

What exactly were you thinking? And be honest.

In no time, Zay was responding.

Your pussy ridin' my face and you grinding on my tongue.

"Damn," Olivia whispered as she quickly sent another message.

What are you still up doing? The old man must be gone for the night?

She responded back with an unsure smile. She didn't even want to mention her husband to Zay anymore, not knowing how he'd acted.

He is gone for the night. He'll return in the morning.

Zay wasted no time replying.

I should've been there to hold you.

66

Olivia felt fuzzy inside.

Yes, you should've been.

About five minutes had passed with no response back then finally, Zay said something else.

It was good hearing from you. I'm glad you're well. I was just missing you. I have to fall back a little because I've gotten in too deep.

Olivia's sad face returned. She thought that they were back making progress. She was, just that quickly, not interested in her husband again. She hurriedly messaged Zay back.

It doesn't have to be this way.

Zay responded back.

It does while you're married. I guess we both know what that means.

Olivia didn't know how to feel about that. She was married. He knew that and now she felt like he was giving her an ultimatum. She'd known her husband for eight years. She'd only known him for three months. She quickly messaged him back and then closed down her computer...

I'm sorry you feel that way. Good Night

The next morning Olivia woke up to her cell phone ringing. She reached over on the nightstand and answered it.

"Hello," she said sounding half sleep.

"Wake your ass up," Zoe said on the other end of the phone.

"Do you know what time it is?" Olivia asked, looking at the time on the alarm clock next to her bed. It showed 7:30a.m.

"It's time for you to get up. Look," she started. "My birthday is Saturday and I have tickets to the hottest party in the city that night and I want you to go. Be prepared to stay the night in Atlanta with me that night. Go ahead and let your husband know what the deal is."

Olivia sat up, and rubbed her eyes. "Girl, you know mom is cooking this big dinner for you on Sunday and you talking about staying the night in Atlanta Saturday night. How the hell are we supposed to party all night Saturday and you still show up for your Birthday dinner on time."

"Because, you're going to drive us back and then I'll stay the night at mom's and leave on Tuesday or Wednesday." She said.

"Knowing you and mom's relationship, you'll probably be leaving on Monday morning." They laughed. "I'll be home in the morning though, because she wants to take me shopping and to the spa for a mother daughter day out as a starter for my birthday."

"She has always been good for our mother daughter pre-birthday dates. Those are the only times that I've ever saw her unwind a little and relax. I believe she looks forward to the days leading up to our birthdays."

"I believe she do, too." Zoe laughed. "Well, tell Felisha to be ready on Saturday night too, because we're gonna have us a ball."

"Well, I don't know if she'll be up for going. She and I had a few words yesterday while we were out eating lunch."

"A few words," Zoe said, knowing that the two of them never fell out with each other. "What brought that on?"

"Honestly, I don't know. It started with her making jokes about Sly standing me up on our wedding day."

Zoe frowned. "Why would she want to trip about something that serious? You were really broken up over that. Plus, that was back when you were twenty-three years old. It took you a good two years to get over it and I don't believe you'd still be over it if Mark hadn't showed up. That's who came along and mended your broken heart."

"He did that and waited until we got married to sleep with me. He respected my body and my wishes of waiting."

"Yeah, see he is a good one," Zoe said, "But, he probably waited, because even though you were the virgin; he probably was one too, how he carry on some shameful in the bedroom." They laughed out loud.

"I just can't get over her bringing up that wedding back then to Sylvester. Why would she even want to bring that up?" Zoe didn't like anybody picking at her sister, not even if it was Felisha.

"I don't know. She even spoke about mom being strict on us and how my marriage is now over."

"Why'd she say that?"

"Because," Olivia said, not wanting to say it.

"Oh, because you're fucking around with Zay?" She asked, already knowing about Zay since Olivia told her everything.

"That had to be it. I don't know what her problem was, but I believe that for the first time in our friendship, I sensed jealousy. I don't know where it came from, but an attitude was mixed in with it."

"Maybe she's just mad because now you have two men vying for your attention and she can't get one man to stay around long enough to vie for hers."

"I don't know, but I hate we had that disagreement. I'm not even going to mention the party to her. I think she needs to think about what really happened. She owes me an apology."

"Well, y'all will work that out. Y'all have been friends for way too long to let something petty come between y'all. Plus, I don't care if she doesn't come with us Saturday night. As long as you're there then I'm good."

"Well, I'm going to be there," Olivia confirmed.

"Good, and we'll talk more about Zay when I see you tomorrow. I'm actually excited about coming home for a change. It's been a few months now and I miss you."

"I miss you, too. I can't wait until you get here. We have lots of catching up to do." She said, and then after a few more minutes of small talk, they ended their call.

Minutes later, Olivia could hear the front door open as the house alarm sounded off. She then heard the four beeps coming from Mark putting in their code to turn it off. She smiled, feeling good to know that her husband had made it home. He walked through their bedroom door with a smile on his face.

"Hey babe, I thought you would still be sleeping since this is your late day to go in the salon."

"Hey honey," she spoke back. "I would've been sleep, but I just hung up with Zoe. You know her birthday is Saturday and she wants me to go out with her Saturday night in Atlanta."

"Saturday night? I guess you'll be staying the night, because you know you're not driving that far back home and I know you're going to be drinking."

"Well, babe those were the plans." She assured him. She got out of bed and walked over to him in her short lace, silk slip that she slept in. She didn't waste any time unbuckling his pants and going straight for his dick. Mark was a bit shocked.

"You must've really missed me," he teased.

Once his boxers and pants were down around his ankles, Olivia started sucking his dick.

"Damn," he said taking in a deep breath. Olivia had to make herself back up off of him or he would know that she'd been taking lessons on a different dick. She was surprised that he even let her go that far. She had never tasted him before and he was actually better tasting than she imagined as she slurped him just a little longer before he stopped her.

Mark then bent her over on the edge of the bed. He stepped out of his pants and boxer shorts and stood back to get a good view of his wife's hot pussy as it sat out from the back waiting for some direct contact from his anxious dick.

He stepped up and entered inside her world. Olivia took in a deep breath as Mark slowly entered her from the back. He started pumping deeper and deeper, making her moan like he'd never heard before. Her pussy was sloppy wet and begging for his attention and he was giving it to her. She was surprised that he was going in the way he was. He stopped fucking her then slipped his tongue in her pussy.

"Oh shit," Olivia said, feeling her knees buckle. Mark was really being a bad boy. He'd never put his mouth on her goods before, but now he was showing off. She took in a deep breath, feeling him slide his dick back inside her and as soon as it was getting really good, he turned her back over on her back.

"Nooooo," she said.

"Yessss," Mark said, and then he fucked her for about five more minutes in missionary style before cumin'.

Damn, Olivia thought as she lay there feeling cheated, yet again.

Chapter Thirteen

"Zay," Dillon called out. "Get yo ass up!"

Zay covered his head with a pillow. "Man, get outta my room. Didn't I just see you yesterday? I'm tired."

"Nigga your ass is a NFL agent. You don't do shit all day but sit in your office and talk on the phone. Oh and play around on Twitter, Instagram, Facebook and shit."

"It's more to my job than that and I believe you know it."

"Quit griping man. You should be in a good mood." Dillon said, snatching the pillow off Zay's head. "Get yo ass up."

Zay rolled over on his back "Damn man, I just showered and laid down good and here you go. You'll fuck up a wet dream." He grumbled. "Think I'ma need to get that key back from your ass."

"You won't be thinking about no key after I tell you what I got."

Zay rubbed his eyes with an anxious look. "What the hell you got?"

"I got those VIP tickets for us."

"What VIP Tickets?"

"You know what tickets." Dillon grinned.

"Not those tickets," Zay said in hopes that it was *those tickets.*

Dillon pulled the tickets out of his back pocket. "Yeah Buddy... THOSE TICKETS," he slowly said fanning the tickets in the air with a wide smile on his face.

Zay smiled from ear to ear. "Damn man," he said. "You for real?"

"Don't these look real?" Dillon asked, putting a ticket in Zay's face.

Zay started cheesing. "We finally lucked up and got some tickets. I need to find something to wear to this party. What's the theme this year?"

Dillon looked at the ticket. "It says, *Mask Your Pleasures.* It seems to be a masquerade theme."

"Masquerade theme, you say?" Zay asked, already thinking about what he'd wear.

"Bro, do you know how many women are gonna be there?"

"YESSSSS," Zay said. "This is the muthafuckin party of the year."

"Hell, it's the only party of the year. This shit won't go down again until next year."

"And, you got us in there. How did you get the tickets, Bro?"

"So check this." Dillon started. "I was having an early morning meeting with Romello about booking a few shows locally," he said, speaking of his business partner. "He was sittin' there talking to me about how he'd gotten these tickets for his birthday a few months ago, but realized that he wouldn't be able to go due to something else coming up. He pulls out the tickets and hands them to me. You know I went wild when I saw *Mask Your Pleasures.* There is only one party that goes down once a year and it's a no holds barred celebration of skin against skin. No telling what the hell we gonna see there." He coolly grinned.

"You right about that. I bet it's gonna be some freaky ass women in the place."

"Yeah, even if they don't wanna fuck nothing; they're still there to see some kind of action."

"You're right," Zay said, thinking that any woman there had to have a high sex drive or some kind of freak in them. And whatever the freak o'meter read, it had to definitely be at a high level.

"It's gonna be held at a mansion with fifteen bedrooms, I heard. Romello went two years ago and said it was off the chain. It was private rooms where people could go fuck and open areas where people were just having orgies. This year is really going to be crazy being that you have to wear masks. You can't enter without a mask and these tickets are only for the elite. Hell, the person that bought them for Romello, paid three hundred dollars a ticket."

"Damn, I know he hate that he is going to miss this shit this year." Zay then smiled. "But I sho' thank him!"

"Yeah, because the tickets are so hard to come by," Dillon said. "That's why I hurried up and jumped on them. We may never get a chance to hit a party like this again."

"You ain't lying." Zay said with a smile on his face that wouldn't go away.

"I think we need to get out so I can find a good mask to wear." Zay said, already scheming. Going to this party would be a big distraction from Olivia and he needed a serious distraction from her. It was crazy, because he'd been dreaming about her sexy body before his brother woke him up. He wasn't lying about him fucking up a wet dream.

"I'm just gonna find a black mask and put on something simple, but dressed for the occasion. You definitely can't go up in there in no sneakers and white tees."

"I kinda figured that," Zay responded. He got out of bed. "I need to get my shit together. Are we going to find something to wear? I just need me a fresh mask that hides who I am, but still add to my swag." He said as Dillon jumped on his laptop. He figured his brother was going to be awhile, so he may as well pull up his Twitter account and make himself useful.

"You talk to your girl?" Dillon asked, as he began to surf the web first.

Zay stepped inside his big closet, looking for some clothes he could put on. "Yeah, I hit her up last night. I just wanted to check on her."

"And how'd that make you feel?"

"I don't even know. I can't lie, I'm drunk over her ass." He admitted.

"Hell, I know that." Dillon said. "This party may be just the thing to help you get your mind right. I think you've been missing out these past couple of months."

"I don't call it missing out, because she makes up for four or five women by herself. I just can't be this drunk over her knowing that she has a husband."

"Hell, I feel you," Dillon said, scrolling through his newsfeed on Twitter. "Well, it seems that she's up and about to meet with her bestie for an early morning breakfast at IHop."

"How you know that?"

"Twitter," he answered. "It tells you everything you need to know. It's like a free GPS on everybody you fuck with. You'll always know their whereabouts." They laughed.

"You right about that," Zay responded. He'd hated hearing about her, because now he wanted to hear her voice. "I need to do better," he whispered while searching through his things. He found a casual pair of Rocawear khakis and a Pipe 2 Rocawear t-shirt. He pulled out a new pair of khakis Roc Moc's that he'd bought six months earlier, but didn't have anything to wear with them.

Dillon glanced up from the laptop as he checked out Zay's gear. "Aye I got the black ones just like those."

"Yeah, I do too." Zay grinned, and then stepped inside his master bathroom to clean up. Twenty minutes later, he walked out and looked over at Dillon. "You ready boy?"

"There are only two types of boys in this world; a white boy and a cowboy. Don't ever forget that." Dillon joked as he logged out of his Twitter account and closed the top on the laptop. He got up to walk out of Zay's room then looked back as he made it to the door. "And clean up this damn place. That woman got you gone."

Olivia sat inside the IHOP at a booth seat, waiting for Felisha to show up. She couldn't believe that they'd had such a fucked up falling out. Felisha was saying some really low shit and she didn't appreciate it. However, she was grown enough to overlook it and she was hoping that Felisha would feel the same.

Felisha walked up and gave Olivia a somewhat salty hug. "Hey," she dryly spoke.

"Hey," Olivia said, still trying to be the bigger person since it didn't look like Felisha wanted to take a try at it. "You okay?"

"Yeah I'm good," she coolly responded.

"About yesterday," Olivia started. "I think we both said some pretty hurtful things, but I'd like to apologize. I don't know where that came from or why it started, but I'm sorry." She sincerely said then she tried to spice up the conversation so that Felisha wouldn't even have to apologize. "Girl, Mark fucked me from the back this morning. It was so good." She bragged.

Felisha frowned as she sat across from her best friend still feeling some type of way. "I don't want to hear about your sex life this morning." She bluntly stated then carried on. "I honestly didn't like the way you spoke of me fucking around with Tom, Dick, and Harry on yesterday."

"I didn't say that. You just did." Olivia cut in.

"You know what I'm talking about." Felisha said with a slight roll of the neck. "And to mention my son's father and what he doesn't do for him in front of my son was definitely not called for."

"Are you still serious right now? You joked off of me being a virgin and being left at the altar. You said some pretty hurtful shit to me, too and you're just gonna sit here in my face and make me feel like the bad guy? That's fucked up."

"You're right, it is fucked up. I hate we're sitting here arguing over something so stupid, but it was some things said that I took straight to the heart. I'm sitting here feeling like you've been feeling that way about me forever." Felisha said, looking pitiful with a pissed off attitude.

Olivia disappointedly shook her head. "I can't believe we're having this discussion."

"Yesterday showed me another side of you, a side that I don't like."

"Girl, you are really tripping right now. We've been best friends since we were around four years old. You're like my sister."

Felisha sat there looking like she didn't even care. "I just have some things to think about."

"Things like what?"

"I just need to figure some things out in my life."

Olivia looked confused. "Like what?"

"You said something yesterday that really got to me. You said that I've never been married or engaged and that shit hurt because I could've been."

"Why do you keep saying that shit?" Olivia asked with frustration in her tone. "Are you referring to the guy that you wanted to introduce to me after I told you that I wanted you to meet Mark?"

"Yep," Felisha said.

"But--" Olivia said then was cut off.

"But, my so called man decided at the last minute to take a different route."

Olivia nodded her head. "Right, he didn't show up. You said at the last minute, he got cold feet about just being in a relationship. So, how did that ever lead up to you marrying him?" Olivia curiously asked.

"Because after the fact, he did come back and he told me that he wanted to be with me." Felisha said. "He even told me that he'd marry me."

"Oh and you turned that down?" Olivia smugly asked.

"I did, for my own personal reasons. I deserve more than a man that just walks out on me like that, but it's been plenty of times I should've just gone with the flow. If I had gone with the flow then we would be married and my son would have a father around twenty-four, seven."

"If you think it's that easy then kid yourself, because it's not. And I guarantee you that if he couldn't show up just so your best friend could meet him, talking about not wanting a commitment then he wasn't trying to marry you."

Felisha stood up from the table. "I'm about to go," she said with tears in her eyes.

"What is wrong with you?" Olivia asked.

"Nothing that I can't handle," Felisha responded. "Are you still going to be able to take lil Romeo to the dentist tomorrow?"

"Yes, I'll be by to get him in the morning. Are you going to be alright?" Olivia asked out of concern. "I worry about you, sometimes."

"That's good to know," Felisha said with a slight smile. "We'll catch up later." She said, giving Olivia a slight hug, and with that, she left.

Later that night, Olivia and Mark lay in bed having pillow talk. It was a part of her that wanted to work on her marriage. The only problem was shaking Zay. As she lay there having this sweet conversation with her husband, her thoughts were still on another man. She quickly tried to talk about something different to clear her mind of Zay.

"I met with Felisha today," she said.

"How'd that go?" Mark asked, already hearing about their earlier fallout.

"I don't know what's wrong with her. She is acting all strange and shit."

"What do you mean?" Mark asked with a slight frown on his face.

"She's acting jealous or something. She even brought up that time when that dude she was screwing around with was supposed to meet with us."

"Huh," Mark said like he unaware of what time she was talking about.

"Remember when I first introduced you to Felisha?"

Mark nodded. "Oh yeah, I remember that, but her man didn't show up."

"Right," Olivia said. "He didn't even have the courtesy to show up, but she telling me that he wanted to marry her."

"Well, what happened? Why didn't they get married?"

Olivia shook her head. "Baby, that's the same thing I was thinking, but she claimed that after he didn't show up, he came back to her house wanting to be with her. I guess that's when he said that he'd marry her."

"What stopped it then?"

"She said that she didn't take him back for her own personal reasons."

Mark sat silent for a moment. "That sounds crazy."

"It does," Olivia agreed. "Maybe you should talk to her for me. She might feel more comfortable talking to you now since she and I have this elephant in the room anytime we're around each other."

"Yeah, I understand. I don't mind talking to her to see if she'll open up. I don't need her going off the deep end. We've made a good investment with her." He joked, but was very serious.

Olivia grinned. "You're right about that." They laughed, and then talked a little more before dozing off to sleep.

Chapter Fourteen

The next day, Olivia and Zoe sat in the massage chairs, getting a pedicure as Mrs. Jackson sat on the other end of the nail salon getting a fresh polish with French tips. Olivia looked over at Zoe and smiled. She was happy that her kid sister was home.

"So, what's up with you?" Olivia asked with a big smile on her face. "I've missed you kid."

Zoe laughed. She loved her sister and even though she was only two years younger, Olivia would call her kid from time to time.

"I've missed you, too." Zoe responded, smiling back just as big. "You know mom wasn't going to let me stay away another month longer, anyway. She would've either put out an APB out on me or she would've just showed up on my doorstep one day and ain't nobody got time for that."

Olivia laughed. "You got that right." She said, looking down at her controlling, obsessive mother and smiled with a shake of the head. "That's mom."

"Yep, that's her and I don't need her snooping around at my crib trying to regulate. I'm single and I live like a single woman. My place is colorful, with modern décor. I even have naked people hanging on the wall."

Olivia laughed. "You have what now?"

"Yes, you heard right. I live freely now and it feels good." She glanced down on the other end of the nail salon to make sure that Mrs. Jackson wasn't finished yet then she kept talking. "It's crazy when I think back at how we lived. Don't get me wrong, because we had the best of everything, but we lived like lil rich slaves."

Olivia wanted to laugh, but she held it in. "I guess I can agree to that."

"You know you can." Zoe cut in. "We grew up with white carpet that stayed white. You better not walk your ass in there with shoes on. They better come off at the door and your feet or socks better be clean."

Olivia nodded with a smile, because she knew that her sister wasn't lying as she continued.

"Mom doesn't have a bright anything in that house. It's either beige or a dull gray or something. Walking in that house every day almost felt like I was checking myself in an upscale psyche ward."

Olivia chuckled.

"We had a big five bedroom house with four full baths and every inch of that house was immaculate."

Olivia nodded her head, quickly agreeing with her sister. "You are absolutely right. You could eat your food off of the floor in that house." Zoe laughed at her comment. "No, but you're right. Mom was no joke and the sad part is that she's still the same mom and the house is just as spotless as it was thirteen years ago when I lived there."

"Sure is," Zoe responded. "Mom won't change a thing, but I'm going to get her to change the color in the kitchen eventually. She has gotta start somewhere. I'm working on her."

"If anybody can do it you can," Olivia said, feeling that she and their dad were always the closest, but Zoe had a special bond with their mom. It may not have looked like it, but they did.

Zoe was the very smart and sassy one. She looked exactly like their mom with the smooth, chestnut colored skin and long hair half way down their backs. Zoe had the Asian looking, dreamy eyes too, which were the only thing that Olivia got from their mom, because everything else resembled their dad. Olivia's big white smile and high cheek bones with the perfect pouty lips were a spitting image of Mr. Jackson, as well as, the smooth, chocolate glow of her skin tone.

Zoe was resentful for a lot of things that Mrs. Jackson made them do. She hated taking summer courses when they'd already passed their grades. She hated ten o'clock curfews still at the age of eighteen. She hated the boring, but very expensive décor in the home. But, most importantly, she hated the promise of not being able to lose her virginity until she'd gotten married. She could've gone against the grain and slept with a guy, but she didn't. However, she did marry this curly head, hottie name Chico during her sophomore year in college just because she was ready to fuck. Nothing heated their mom more.

"So, does it feel good to be single again?" Olivia asked, wiggling her toes in the warm water.

"Sure does," Zoe answered. "I just wished I would've waited before I jumped right into another relationship after Chico and I separated. I was married by the age of twenty-one and split up by the age of twenty-eight. Then my crazy ass goes against mom's wishes and shacks with another man for another two years; only for that shit to crumble, too. What the hell was I thinking?"

"That's just how it is sometimes." Olivia said.

"No, but we both know that mom is crazy, but she ironically has decent logics," Zoe admitted. "She did stay on our asses in hopes of us attending college first while only looking to the men who didn't pressure us of wanting nothing more than a friendship, and then she was sure that things would grow and take form from there."

"Build on your foundation is what she'd say," Olivia cut in. "I think we both made the same mistake with our first loves. I mean, Sylvester swept me off of my feet in high school. He was the sexiest nigga I'd ever laid eyes on. He was very popular and the most skilled quarterback on the football team in high school and college."

Zoe nodded then chimed in. "And you were the pretty girl, the homecoming queen and the head cheerleader that all the boys wanted. You and Sly were destined to be together back then. He did love you. I always felt like he was infatuated with not only your looks, but your morals. That's why he stayed so long. He wanted to be the first one to get what all the guys couldn't and he was in the perfect position to be able to get it."

"Yeah, and it did me no good to try to give it to him, either. I struggled with that night, but because we were getting married in two days, I was like what the hell. It seemed the closer we got to our wedding the more he'd be in my ear about just wanting to feel my insides and see what it'd be like before the wedding and I gave in like a dummy."

"Almost gave in, because technically he didn't pop that cherry." Zoe teased, but was very serious.

"If he wasn't so big, it would've worked." Olivia said kind of feeling embarrassed at the moment that she couldn't satisfy the one man that she wanted more than anything in the world back then. I probably would've been married to him right now still."

"That's not necessarily true now, because I did wait with Chico and we're not together now. The truth with that though, is that we married too young. Neither one of us was ready for that. Hell, if you ask me, we both just wanted to fuck. He still, hands down, has the best dick I've ever had."

"You've only had five." Olivia joked.

Zoe popped her lips and playfully rolled her eyes. "And you're the one to talk with only two under your belt."

"Almost three," Olivia quickly corrected.

"Yeah almost," Zoe said with a chuckle. "But seriously, I was the cause of me and Chico going our separate ways. I'd become mom," she admitted. "I became this neat freak, making my husband come out his shoes when he'd walk in the door. It makes me cringe when I think back at how controlling I'd become." She said with a disappointing shake of the head as she continued.

"It was like I'd become jealous of his career and shit. I mean, the man is a producer. He makes really good money, working with different artists."

"A lot of them being women, too," Olivia added.

"Yep, and I had a problem with that. My husband looks good and women these days are thirstier than nigga's if you ask me."

"True," Olivia said.

"I started hounding him. Showing up to his place of business and shit like I was crazy," Zoe said. "I was doing the most and all he was doing was providing us with a secure, stable living. I'd hear people say that he wouldn't cheat on me, because I was so pretty and smart, but let's just keep it real. I don't care how pretty and fine you are, if your nigga wanna layup with another bitch then trust and believe that he will."

"You ain't never lied." Olivia chimed in with a light chuckle. "We shouldn't have been so hot in the ass. That would've saved us from the earlier heartbreaks."

Zoe shook her head. "I think we both went against the grain back then when we should've just taken Dr. Jackson's advice."

"Yeah, because she begged us both to wait and love would find us."

"She kills me with the philosopher shit, though." Zoe cut in then looked at the Chinese lady doing her toe nails. "Aye, take it easy on that toe. You just nicked me."

The Chinese lady quickly apologized. "I'm sorry," she said.

She looked back over at her sister, shaking her head like she wanted to slap the Chinese lady. "Anyway, I think that if mom had let us make our own decisions and not pressure us into so many things then we would be fine. I gotta admit it though. Good sex stretched both of my relationships or it they would've been over."

Olivia laughed. "I think I know exactly how you feel on that one. Good sex will not only lengthen a bad relationship, but it can also hook your ass into believing it's something good when it's not," she said, now thinking about Zay's good dick ass. "If only I was getting good dick at home. I would be fine."

"Is things still dull on the home front?" Zoe asked.

"Girl, I thought Mark was about to give it to me yesterday morning, but it turned right on back into the same old, tired thang. I can hardly deal with that anymore. The thrill has been long gone. I love him, but I'm not in love with him and quite frankly I don't know if I still wanna be there."

"Damn, and Mark is one of the good ones."

"Well, technically he's not that good," Olivia joked as they laughed. "Now Zay on the other hand, is off the chain with it. However, he no longer wants to be with me either, because of Mark. Ain't that something how the man I'm drunk in love with is throwing me an ultimatum, but there's nothing I can do about it at the moment."

Zoe disappointedly shook her head. "Damn," she whispered. "That shit is crazy. Well, look... We are not about to get sidetracked. Tomorrow is my birthday and I just want to spend it with my sister and enjoy the night. Is Felisha gonna make it? I got her covered if she wants to go."

"Nah, I asked her this morning when I took lil Romeo to the dentist for her."

"Oh, she doesn't want to party? She never misses out on a good party."

"Well, she's missing out on this one. She's going through some things right now. I don't know what the hell it could be. Maybe she's feeling some type of way about not being settled down by now."

"What happened to the baby daddy?" Zoe curiously asked.

"He still never comes around. It pisses me off, because he doesn't know what he's missing out on. That lil boy is so smart and cute. I guess I take that a lil personal, because I'm his God mom and or auntie as he calls me, but I take on the role as his father. Hell, me and Mark are always babysitting or looking out for her when it comes to him."

"I know." Zoe said, thinking that Olivia had been there since day one when lil Romeo was born. "He's just the cutest thing. I feel like his auntie too, because that's how much you had him as a baby and even now."

"I know and Felisha knows that I love her. Mark talked me into investing some of our money in her nail salon to help her get established so she could take care of her son without a man. I was glad he had that talk with me, because she ain't about to get no man, no time soon." She bluntly stated. "I just don't see it."

"But, she wants a man." Zoe cut in.

"And I can believe it. I feel that has been definitely bothering her, lately. Unlike us, she has a kid and by a man that obviously wants no dealings with her or her son. That's gotta be tough. Plus, I'm married, an independent business woman, with no kids. Maybe, she's starting to feel a little jealous."

"You know, we women tend to be some very emotional beings and it can take us a long time to get over a man that we were once in love with. Heartache is one of the worse feelings in the world. It doesn't just digest right away. The only way we can sometimes get past that is if someone else comes along and eases that pain. Otherwise, it stays with us. Anyways," she said, having to clear her thoughts off of Chico, the only man she'd ever loved. "Tonight we're gonna enjoy my birthday barbeque since Mom already knows that we won't be making it back by Sunday after partying all night on Saturday."

"I can't wait. I think I need this, too. More than you know. Maybe it'll clear up some of these crazy thoughts I'm having about ending my marriage."

"Well, we don't wanna think about that right now." She said then changed the subject to something more interesting. "I already bought you something to wear to the party."

"What you mean, bought me something?" Olivia asked with a frown. "Is there a dress code or something?"

"Yep, it sure is and I have the perfect thing for you to wear. Just trust me on this, you're gonna love it." Olivia shook her head, because no telling what Zoe had on the agenda for her.

"What kind of party is this we're going to?" she curiously asked.

"Not telling until you get there. You think you're thinking about Zay now. Wait until after this party. No telling what or who you'll be thinking about then. And, you could be right. It might just clear some things up for you concerning your marriage."

Can't say if that will be good or bad, but hell... You never know. Zoe quickly thought then continued.

"I think it's time we both let out hair down. This party is only for the grown and sexy and I do believe that we're grown and sexy." She smiled, causing Olivia to smile back. "And it's only for the elite. I bet nobody there will have a bank account that's under two-hundred thousand."

"You will," Olivia teased with a light chuckle.

"Technically, just short of it. But, as long as our wealthy parents are on top then so am I."

"I know that's right. Now, pleeeeeaaaase tell me more about this party." She begged with a playful pout.

"No ma'am. You shall see in due time." Zoe said with a devious smile on her face.

Chapter Fifteen

Zay and Dillon stood in the elevator, waiting for it to hit the first floor. Both were very anxious and excited about going to this elite masquerade party.

"Man, you got some condoms?" Dillon quickly asked with a cheesy smile on his face.

"I didn't bring any, because I'm not sure if I'm fucking. I might stick my finger in a woman's pussy if she let me, but I don't know about my dick. I'm just going to see what these party's are all about. Every man should attend one of these at least once in their lifetime."

"Well, I can agree," Dillon said. "But, you know me, Bro. I'm going to fuck something." He said looking up at the floor display and seeing the elevator drop down from 9...8...7... "I'm sticking my finger in some pussy and some ass. My tongue is going in some lucky woman's mouth and my dick is gettn' sucked and fucked tonight. I've already popped an ecstasy pill and all, Bro. I'm telling you, I am about that life."

"I see," Zay said with a light chuckle, thinking that he was always the promiscuous one that loved fucking woman, but Dillon might've had him beat.

3...2...1... The elevator eased to a complete stop as the doors opened.

"Touchdown," Dillon said, stepping off of the elevator like he and his brother were celebrities.

Zay glanced over at him. "Maybe I'm a little underdressed." He said, peeking at Dillon's fresh, Digital Barocco print shirt, a black pair of Leather Embellished jeans both by Versace. His footwear consisted of a pair of black, high top Barocco sneakers as he stepped with swag pushing his Cartier brown lens sunglasses up on his face.

"I thought you said that we couldn't wear sneakers." Zay said as they headed out of the lobby doors.

"These aren't just any sneakers. These are Versace's that cost fourteen hundred dollars. They better recognize." Dillon coolly said, walking in front of his brother, and then easing his shades down as he winked at a cute chick that was passing by. "Plus, you ain't looking too Shabby now, Bro."

Zay looked down at his attire. He was indeed fresh to death in his Gucci gear from head to toe. "Yeah, well I guess you're right." He said, feeling pretty good. He'd even picked out the perfect mask to match it.

"You driving?" Dillon asked Zay as they got closer to his car. "We can go in the Bentley. That should definitely turn heads."

"Nah," Zay said, passing his Bentley. "We'll go in the Camaro tonight." He said, admiring the sleek, jet black whip that had also turned plenty of heads his way. If nothing else, he always knew that an expensive new car was a woman magnet off top.

"Sounds good to me," he said as Zay hit the unlock button for them to get inside the car.

On the drive over to the party, the brothers talked. "Damn, Bro I'm feeling giddy as fuck. This party is a no holds barred, an anything goes type of showdown."

"I know, man. I've been geeked since I saw the tickets." Zay responded.

"I heard it's going to be a freak fest of games being played and plenty of free alcohol to get you right. Ain't nothing more exciting than that, except a bunch of horny women walking around ready for whatever."

"Come on, Bro. Every woman that'll be there don't wanna fuck. You just have some people that are curious. They might wanna see other people fuck, but not join them. They may just wanna get a high off of the shit, and then go home and fuck, but I'm sure everybody ain't there to fuck. I know I ain't." Zay said as Dillon cut his eyes over at him. "I ain't just gonna stick my dick inside the first broad who comes my way. One thing I'm used to is pussy. I gotta be feeling this chick in some kind of way or my dick won't even get hard."

Dillon frowned. "Damn man, you ain't supposed to be feeling nobody like that. You're supposed to be fucking something, not sizing up ass and how a bitch looks. Fuck that! They gonna have on masks anyway. Pussy don't have a face."

"Nah, fuck what you're talking about," Zay said. "I don't get turned on like that. She gotta have some spunk about her, some business, a bit of sassy mixed with a little bit of sexy in her swag to make a nigga wanna fuck something."

"If you say so, but you know me... This shit is right up my alley. I don't get feelings, I don't know what emotions are and I damn sho' ain't crazy about attachments. All I wanna do is strap up, fuck and move on; nothing more, nothing less." Dillon explained, feeling pretty good from the ecstasy pill he'd popped and the three shots of Patron he drowned it with.

"That's why you're buying new tires every other week, dumb ass. You gon' fuck around and start losing respect from these women." Zay said.

"Does it look like I care about all that?" Dillon questioned. "I love being single and it ain't like I lie to them. I let all women know what time it is upfront."

"Okay, I hear ya pimpin'." Zay said as he pressed the brakes, suddenly slowing the car down. "Is this the place?" He asked, pulling up to the gated security booth.

"Yeah, it better be unless we put the wrong address in the GPS."

A red head black woman walked out of the security booth and over to the window of the car. "I think we're at the right place." Zay said, looking at her sexy attire. She had on a short ruffled baby doll dress with the thigh high stockings and a pair of Black Red Bottoms. Her breasts were so big that they were about to pop out.

"Nice ride," she said with a smile then leaned down to speak directly face to face with the men. "Do you handsome men have your VIP tickets?" Her breast was creeping out of her dress. She rubbed the side of Zay's face with the back of her rough hand as if to entice him with her seductive look, but it wasn't working. He looked over at her and smiled, but wished like hell that Dillon would hurry up and hand her the tickets. She wasn't turning him on the least bit with all that messy red lipstick smeared across her lips.

Dillon opened up the glove compartment. "My bad sweetie, I forgot I put them in here." He said, reaching over Zay and handing her the tickets.

She scanned over their tickets and smiled. The she snapped her fingers at the other person inside the booth and the large gate began to slowly open. "Follow the brick road all the way around to the mansion. Valet attendants will park your car for you. Y'all have fun and holla back at me if you get bored." She said.

Zay smiled with a nod of his head and pulled off in a hurry. "Did you see her?"

"She wasn't that bad man." Dillon commented.

"The hell she wasn't," he said. "She should've had on her mask. The Lady looks like a dude with red hair and big titties."

"Yeah, she should've had her mask on, though." He joked with a light chuckle.

"If the other women here look like her then I'm sure I won't be staying long."

Dillon shook his head. "I'm sure you're gonna change your mind once we get inside this big ass house. Plus, they should have on their masks." His mouth dropped open as he stared at the enormous house. "Damn! Look at this big bitch." He said as they pulled around in front of it. The valet attendant walked over to the car just as the woman at the front gate told them.

Zay looked over at Dillon before they stepped out of the car. "I sho' hope the hype is what it's pumped up to be."

"Don't worry, Bro. Once you get a drink or four in your system you'll relax more. Now quit complaining and get out the damn car. I thought you were excited about this." Dillon stated as he happily got out the car and walked straight into the house. Zay followed closely behind him not knowing what the hell he'd signed up for, but hopefully the party would at least clear his thoughts about wanting to see Olivia.

Olivia sat on the passenger side of the car feeling pretty good as she looked over at Zoe who was driving.

"Zoe, why in the hell didn't you tell me this shit before we left the house?" She asked.

"Because I knew you wouldn't have wanted to come." Zoe answered with a smile. "I'm not coming to get buck wild, but I'm personally curious to see what kind of kinky shit goes on at these things."

"What if somebody sees me here and tells Mark."

"O', we're in Atlanta, who in the hell else is going to be at this party that knows your boring husband? Plus, you're gonna be wearing that cute lil mask in your lap. You know the one that matches that pretty, one shoulder, satin with the lace ruffles, baby doll dress you're wearing."

"Oh, you're talking about this cute lil thing that I'm wearing, huh?" Olivia questioned. "The one with my ass about to hang out," she added, but deep down she loved the dress and the look.

"Yep and don't forget I paid good money for that lil sexy attire. You gotta know I love you, because I bought you something for my birthday."

"Only because you wanted me to accompany you to this freaky ass party," Olivia responded.

"Don't you think we're cute dressed alike?"

"Don't remind me," Olivia grinned.

"I love it. Your dress is red and mine is canary yellow. If they weren't so short, I bet mom would've loved seeing us in these. The lil masks are too cute, too. She added, looking at the sparkles and rhinestones outlining the masks, making them pop even more. "You said that you needed this getaway, right?"

"You know what Zoe, you're right. I did say that I needed this." Olivia said, turning up the small bottle of Patron that was sitting in her lap. Wine was normally the only thing she drank, but she'd said fuck it, so fuck it. "I'm having fun tonight!"

"Good, because we've made it to our destination," Zoe said, pulling up to the security booth.

Olivia smiled, and then noticed the red head lady walk out of the security booth. "She needs a new wig. That red thing on her head ain't hittin' on shit." Olivia commented as they laughed out loud, and then she then turned up some more of the Patron.

"She needs on a mask, too. Shhh... here she comes." Zoe said, letting the window down and shaking her head at Olivia who was now taking another shot of Patron straight out the bottle. "Take it easy with that Patron Sis. That shit will have you fucked up."

"Hey ladies, VIP tickets please." The woman happily said. Zoe handed her the two tickets. The lady scanned over them and signaled for the gate to open. "Follow the brick road and valet will assist you with parking your car. Have fun!" She excitedly said.

"Thanks," Zoe said as she drove off. Two minutes later, they were pulling up in front of the mansion.

Olivia's eyes widened as she saw the mansion. "Damn, this place is huge." Valet stepped up to the 750 big body BMW, waiting for them to get out. Olivia looked over at Zoe and smiled. "Well, it's either now or never."

"I call for now," Zoe said, opening up her car door as she and Olivia got out at the same time. Valet drove off in the car to go park it as they stood in front of the mansion, mouths partly open from the sight of the lit up place.

Olivia started grinning like a kid in a candy store. "No telling what the hell is going on in this bitch!" She said as the cars were lined up with people and the valet parkers were taking their bad ass rides to a safe location to park them. "What are we standing here for?"

"I don't know, but you only turn thirty one once in your life and I came here to party!"

"Well, me too," Olivia chimed in as she led the way.

"Oh shit! Look at her bad ass!" Zoe chimed in, following close behind her sister. Neither knew what to expect, but they anticipated having a very entertaining night as they walked up to the door and was greeted by two women in lingerie pieces and cute lil masks covering their faces.

"Oh my God!" Olivia blurted out while scoping out the action going on between all the friendly, touchy-feely, half naked people. "I think we may have overdressed." She said, looking back at Zoe with a smirk on her face.

Chapter Sixteen

Stepping inside the mansion was like stepping inside a large freak fest. This was the HOTTEST party of the year. The place was beautiful with crystal chandeliers and huge decorative lit candles everywhere. The immaculate abstract furniture was laced with half naked bodies intertwining which made the bunny ranch look like Pee'Wee's Playhouse. The ladies made their way further into the large open area where they spotted a large arc shaped bar and hurriedly made their way to it. A tall, pretty, Spanish bartender greeted them from behind the bar as they approached it.

"Hello ladies and welcome to *Mask Your Pleasures*. I see that this is your first party by the looks on your faces. You may need just a little boost to help you relax." Zoe and Olivia shyly smiled. "We have assorted ways to brighten your horizons and help you relax and enjoy your night. I promise that you'll come back for more."

"Hell, from what I'm seeing, bitches already don't wanna leave." Zoe said, smiling from ear to ear and still looking around scoping the scene out.

"It is different from where we usually go, but damn if it ain't sparking my interest." Olivia surprisingly blurted out. "I wanna take this mask off so I can get a really good look at these people, but I don't want nobody to spot me here."

Zoe was still in awe at the vibrant, sexual feeling that she got just from watching the others enjoying what the other had to offer. Seeing the different masks only made it that more interesting and tantalizing.

"This shit is wild O'. I need a few more drinks to get my head adjusted." She said with a smirk.

"Oh trust me; it's not hard to get your head adjusted in here, sexy." The bartender spoke then winked at Zoe with a seductive smile. "So what would you ladies like to drink before starting your first, and hopefully not your last, sexcapade adventure? Everything is top shelf."

Zoe and Olivia got Patron mixed with a splash of cranberry juice. They both drank two small glasses of it to set the mood right and then decided to walk off, but the bartender stopped them.

"Hey, before you ladies move any further may I interest you in one of our assorted sexual enhancements?" She pulled out a small silver tray from underneath the counter, consisting of various bright colored pills.

The wild child had finally arrived. "Ooooh! HELLZ YEAH! Now this is a damn birthday!" Zoe excitedly stated and with no hesitation... "Let me get the red one. Fuck it, I'm going all in, Sis. Oh and le'me get a straight shot of patron to go. Shiiiiit, it's time to party!" Zoe downed the pill with her shot, motioning a finger at the waitress for one more drink.

"Don't kill yourself in here fool." Olivia chirped, giving Zoe the side-eye.

Zoe hit her lightly on the arm with a wide smile. "Kick back and relax, Sis. What goes on here stays in here."

Olivia sat there looking at the bartender with a crooked, undecided smile on her face. The bartender nudged the tray toward her.

"Don't worry, you'll be fine." She said. "Nothing is going to happen to you. If you relax and don't think about it, you'll have the most fun. You only live once."

"Yeah, but I want that once to last a very, very long time," Olivia stated with an unsure look.

"Girl, if you don't take that damn pill," Zoe politely demanded, almost laughing. "We're here to party."

Olivia didn't need much more convincing. She grabbed the red pill too, which meant if her sister lived, she would too and if she died then they'd die together.

"That's what I'm talking about." Zoe said with a cheesy smile on her face. "Now, let's mingle."

Zoe flirtingly laughed as she eyed one of the half naked male bartenders walking past while pushing the tray of drinks towards her. She shook her head, indicating that she'd had enough for now. She then grabbed Olivia's hand while leading the way down the long marble hallway.

The first open spaced room they passed was filled with men and women having a big ass orgy. The lights were dimmed with a black light effect and the only thing Olivia's eyes were glued to was a man with a big twelve inch dick shooting nut on a woman's face, covering her mask.

"Damn, some of these nigga's are ruined." She said, looking from one big dick to another. "That's why they try to get to parties like this. Ain't nobody else in their right mind is going to fuck them."

Zoe laughed, but seeing all the sucking and fucking was really turning her on. "You crazy, you know that." Olivia playfully shrugged her shoulders. "Let's head on down a lil further." They passed another room door that had a sign on it which read, OCCUPIED. Zoe turned the doorknob anyway, but it was locked. She pulled Olivia by the hand as they passed a woman straddling a man in a chair sitting in the hallway. The woman was giving him the business as his head rested on the back of the chair.

"Damn," Olivia whispered, feeling like she was gliding behind Zoe. Her feet were so light on the floor. The pills and the drinks had obviously kicked in and had her in a cloudy imaginative daze, but a good one. She smiled at the well built men, chilling in their expensive gear as some walked by and smiled. Others were lost in their surroundings, looking like dogs in heat. Next thing Olivia knew, Zoe had her by the hand and was leading her up the stairs.

"Damn it's some fine, thick ass women up in here tonight!" Dillon stated while rubbing his hands together and watching everything moving. "I'm about to find me something to play with. I ain't come here to stand around with you all night soul searching."

"I ain't soul searching, Bro. I'm just still checking this place out. I mean, I've been to plenty of strip clubs, but I ain't used to Nigga's walking around with their dicks hanging out the zipper of their pants." He said, just as a woman walked right over in front of them and grabbed a man's dick and started slurping on it instantaneously.

"Damn," Zay said as he stood there and watched like he was in a live porno movie as a guest observer.

"Hell, I need to walk around with my dick out. From the looks of what I see, the ladies should be standing in line waiting to jerk on this big knob." Dillon said, causing Zay to laugh. "See Bro, you ain't supposed to understand none of this. You just go with the flow and let this place have its way with you." As Dillon explained the concept to Zay he was caught completely off guard by two beautiful, skimpy dressed women that were approaching to past them. They seemed to have walked by them in slow motion as the first woman smirked, throwing up the peace sign as she held on to the woman's hand that followed directly behind her.

"Ladies," Zay and Dillon greeted them in unison, damn near staring them out of their baby doll satin dresses.
A familiar scent swept by Zay's nose as he watched the second woman that was being led from the back as she made it a little further down the hall. "Damn bro, all of a sudden I'm starting to understand what you mean," Zay said still eyeballing the two women till they were out of sight. "Hey uh, you said that you were going to do your thing, right?"

"Damn right," Dillon said, already scoping out the little hottie standing across from him.

"So, hit me on the cell when you're ready. I'm gonna see what this spot got for your boy, and with what just walked passed, it seems to have plenty." He grinned.

"Yeah, I knew you'd see things differently after a while," Dillon chuckled, and then eased off like a sly fox ready to get into something or somebody. Zay set out in the direction of the two women.

Zoe led Olivia into this purple room. The walls were purple, the furniture was purple and purple plush carpet was on the floor. Zoe smiled at just the seductive lure of seeing it all go down like she'd just yelled take two on a bull horn. She was feeling really good as she smiled at an extremely fine ass guy with the tatted up sleeves as he walked over. He had a daring, pearly white smile as he held out his hand.

Zoe looked back Olivia. "Are you good, Sis?"

"Yep," Olivia said, feeling really good herself. "Go have fun. Call me when you're ready to meet up."

Zoe nodded with a smile then grabbed the man's hand and walked off.

There was more mingling going on in that room than anything else. As she stood there swaying her hips to the music as she leaned against the wall just enjoying the scene and like fate, *Drunk In Love* started to play and the next thing she knew, Zay's sweet breath was brushing up on the side of her neck.

"What you doing here?" He asked in her ear.

Olivia shot him a side-eye through the mask. He was wearing a solid black mask trimmed in gold that only covered his eyes as he stared at her, anxiously waiting for a reply.

"What are you doing here?" Olivia asked him back as her heart fluttered from just having him near.

Zay wanted to bend her over and fuck her right there, but he kept the conversation going. "You can't ask a question with a question."

Olivia smacked her lips a little like he was bothering her, but all she was doing was playing hard to get. "It's Zoe's birthday and this is where she brought me to celebrate." She said then moved her head to the music, like he was nobody.

Zay leaned in closer to her ear. He could feel his dick getting hard just standing that close to her and smelling the captivating aroma of her *Dior J'adore* perfume.

"So, is this your type of party?" he asked.

"Nope," she said, still rolling her neck to the music. Her pussy was throbbing anxiously as Zay stood that close to her. She looked over toward him wanting to rip his clothes off, but she held her composure. He could see her seductive, almond shaped eyes behind the mask. She never in a million years thought that he'd be to a party like that, but he was and so was she. "Is this your type of party?"

"Nope," Zay responded. "I'm just here with Dillon."

"Oh," she coolly said then started looking back at the people mingling amongst other things.

Zay was even more turned on by her nonchalant attitude, but he knew it was a front. He could feel her knees shaking the floor beneath him. He smiled to himself knowing that she was caught off guard, but she loved the fact that he was there.

"I've missed you," he said, not able to keep his lips off of her as he kissed her softly on the neck.

Olivia stood there unnerved on the outside, but on the inside her heart had melted at least one hundred times. Zay wasn't there to be playing any games and especially with her. He grabbed her by the hand then led her down the hall. Olivia floated behind him with a smile on her face. It had to be a dream; she was so lost in Lala Land. They passed by one closed door with the *OCCUPIED* sign on it, but Zay kept looking. He was anxious to get her alone so he could do some things to her. Finally nearing the long hallway was a room ducked off around the corner with a *NOT OCCUPIED* sign on the door. Zay opened the door and quickly turned the sign around so that it read now read *OCCUPIED*. He turned to pull Olivia inside the room and once inside it, he locked the door behind them.

Chapter Seventeen

Zay and Olivia had entered another large room with a black light effect that had them looking like they were glowing in the dark. The room was covered with smoke and mirrors along with a black beautiful suede circular sectional that sat in the middle of the floor. Zay wasted no time picking up Olivia and walking her over to the couch. He gently laid her back and then eased his hands down her waist, feeling for her panties. He smiled once he'd made contact with her g-strings. He would've hated to think she was at a party like that with nothing on.

He quickly moved them to the side and dipped his tongue inside her ready goods. Olivia moaned from ecstasy as she let go of herself and allowed him to really go all in.

"Aaaaaaaah.... Mmmmm.... Oooooooh..." She moaned as loud as she could since the sound of her own voice was turning her on and the way Zay's lips touched her lips drove her insane. She grabbed the back of his head as she held it tight. "Pleeeeeaaaase," she said begging for mercy. "Mmmmm.... Oo-oo-oooooh... My Goooooood..." She held his head tighter, grinding her juicy pussy on Zay's anxious tongue. She wanted him to taste it and to eat it all up. He had a mouthful and was going to work.

"Ple-eeee-ase, Oh Pleeeeease..." She called out. "I'm 'bout to cum baby. I'm 'bout to cum."

"Cum in my mouth," Zay aggressively demanded. "Cum in my mouth, baby." He could feel Olivia's grip getting tighter and tighter on his head. This in turn was only making him go harder.

"Oooo-ooooooooH Shit, I'm cumin'!" Olivia let out. "Oooooh, my damn, I'm cumin'." She took in a deep breath then let it out. "It feels so good," she said, feeling the muscles in her pussy pulsating.

Zay stood up, ready to put his big dick inside her. She didn't waste any time opening her legs even wider giving him a personal invite, as Zay slid in deep. He wanted to touch her soul if he could as the walls of her juicy pussy closed in on him, continuing to suck him in.

"Daaaamn," he let out a smooth moan. He stroked her walls, watching the white lube inside her pussy lotion the shaft of his dick. It was the most beautiful thing he'd ever saw and Olivia had the best, cream filled pussy he'd ever had. He could feel her nails digging in his back as he continued to pound away at *his juice box*. He claimed it at the moment, because he knew nobody could put it down like him.

"Yesssssss," she moaned. "This feels so good," Olivia whispered. "I love you, baby. I love you."

Zay heard her and normally he'd respond back, but he was so caught up in a zone that it had his lips sealed and his focus was on pleasing that ass. He kept pumping and pumping her until he felt a tingle in his toes moving up his body. He knew what time it was as he grabbed Olivia's ass cheeks and pulled them closer to him.

He dug deep.

She moaned.

He dug deeper.

She moaned louder.

"You husband can't fuck you like this, can't he?" He questioned as he drilled pleasure inside of her world.

"No, he can't," she admitted, taking in a deep breath. "This dick is good. So-oooo-oo Good," She called out, gripping his back and pulling him closer to her. She wanted to feel all ten inches of his hard rod as she threw it back on it, wanting him to bust one.

With her nails dug deep in his back, his rhythm speeded up and he could tell that he was about to erupt something serious. His snake kept sliding further in as it was going deeper and sliding out longer, until finally, it was pumping mass amounts of venom inside of her. She didn't care as she lay there, because normally they'd use a condom. But, she was taking birth control anyway, so she knew she wasn't pregnant.

Olivia woke up at the crack of dawn with a smile a mile wide spread across her face. Thoughts of being with Zay that night had her gone. He fucked her so good that she woke up playing with herself. He certainly knew how to please her; it was no doubt about that. He was the best thing that had ever come her way and she wanted so badly to be with him, but she was married to a man that had done nothing but been good to her. How in the hell could she possibly leave him? She looked towards the ceiling to have a small chat with the Man above.

"God, I know I've not come to you about anything I've had going on lately." She took in a deep breath. *"That's because I know I've been so wrong in my actions. I don't even know how to talk with you about this now, but it's just so frustrating. I'm in love with another, but I don't want to leave my husband. Well, I do, but why should I? He's good to me and I know he loves me. Either, I'm going to have to shake Zay and make it work with my husband or I'm going to have to serve my husband divorce papers to be with my lover. I know I'm in love with Zay, but what if it's just the lust of loving him. I'm so confused, God. Would you please give me some clarity? If I need to stay with my husband, show me. If I need to leave Zay, show me. In Jesus name I pray. I love you. Amen."*

No sooner than Olivia could finish her prayer, Mark was calling her cell phone. She looked over at the time which displayed seven o'clock in the morning, and then answered her phone.

"What's up, boo?" She answered. "I see somebody's up early."

"Yeah, I tossed and turned last night without you here." Mark stated. She could hear the sincerity in his voice as she slightly smiled.

"Aww, I missed you too." She said, but she knew that it was lie. She was so caught up in Zay's web until she'd forgotten that she was married. He worked her out some kind of good, busting three nuts; two inside of her and one in her mouth.

"When are you coming back home? I miss you. I think we need to have a lil heart to heart." He said.

Olivia sat straight up in bed and rubbed her eyes, at the same time as clearing her throat. "We need to have a heart to heart about what?"

Mark paused then started. "I know that you need more in this relationship." He said, knowing that he'd been short changing her in the bedroom.

Olivia cut in. "You already give me so much," she said, fidgeting with hands, not knowing where he was going with this.

"I know you have needs and I want to be the one that provides you with that; with everything." He said. "I wanna be that man; that all around man that's there for his wife in every way. Whatever you want, just ask and we'll try it, we'll do it, we'll make it work."

Olivia sat quiet for a moment, holding her chest. All the bad shit she'd did with Zay was now crushing her. If only Mark would've said this earlier, he'd still be the only man she would've technically only given herself to.

"You there, baby?" He asked since she was so quiet.

"Uh yeah, babe. I'm here," she responded. "Just hearing you say that to me has truly made me smile. It's so much I want us to do."

"I know," Mark said, feeling like he knew he'd been very selfish with the dick. He knew he had to get it together before he lost his wife. "I promise to be a lot more open minded. Now, when are you coming home? I wanna see you."

"I'm beat, babe. I'm not gonna even lie. You know how my sister is when she gets to celebrating; especially on her birthday."

"Oh, I know." Mark said, feeling like Zoe was more of the wild child, because she'd try or do things that Olivia wouldn't dare do.

"I'll be home on tomorrow morning, though. I miss you, too and I think this heart to heart has been something in the making for a long time."

"I'm glad to hear you admit it." Mark said. "I can't wait to see you. Now, get you some rest and drink plenty of liquids. I know with you being with Zoe you were drinking more than red wine last night.

Olivia laughed, because Mark certainly knew her. "Patron," she said with a shake of the head.

Mark chuckled a little. "Good thing you don't have a hangover. Just get you some rest and call me later."

"Okay," Olivia said. "I love you."

"I know and I love you, too." And with that, they ended their call.

Olivia took the phone from her ear, and then sent Zay a message. It was either now or never and something had to be done. She believed that God was talking to her and she was going to take heed to what he was trying to say.

I need to see you ASAP. O'

Two minutes later, Zay was responding.

I need to see you, too. Come on over."

Olivia read the message and got out of bed. She needed to get dressed, because she and Zay were in for a heart to heart, too. He just didn't know it yet.

Zay sat up in bed with a smile on his face. He couldn't wait to see Olivia. She'd more than carved a place in his heart and he wanted nothing more than to win her over. He understood that she was already in a marriage, but if she was stepping out on her husband then that marriage wasn't working. He wanted her. He needed her and he was going to let it be known when she showed up at his door.

He sat there thinking about what he was going to say to her as his cell phone alerted him of an incoming text. He picked up the cell phone and opened up the message, thinking it was her again. Immediately, he shook his head as he read it.

I was just up this way and wanted to stop by to see you. Miss Good P

Zay instantly knew that was a bad idea; especially with Olivia coming over. He sat there then decided to finally message her back after the one hundred times he'd left her hanging.

Sorry, but I have company

In two seconds flat, she was replying to his message.

What kind of company?

"Is this female for real?" He questioned as he frowned, looking at his phone.

I have someone over. Matter of fact, she's in the bed with me. We'll have to catch up another time.

He sat there for about ten minutes and she never responded. "Good, maybe now she'll get the picture," he said then leaned over and picked up the small square jewelry box that was on his nightstand. Just that quickly his mind was back on Olivia as he smiled, holding on to the box in his hand. A girl's best friends are diamonds and this was something that he learned a long time ago. He opened up the small box, feeling like she would surely love this gift. It was a pair of white gold, diamond earrings with Blossom Motif from a classic collection by Cartier. The ten thousand dollar purchase should definitely let her know that he was in it to win it; all of her and her heart.

"I don't know what her husband is planning on doing, but he better get with the program or he's about to lose her." He said, and then rolled over out of bed, grabbing his robe and heading in the bathroom to shower before Olivia made it there.

An hour and half later, Olivia was knocking lightly on Zay's door. She didn't know how she was going to be able to walk away from such a fun and exciting relationship. One that seemed to keep her in the best of spirits with a guy she'd grown very fond of in just three months time.

Zay opened the door with a smile on his face. "Hey sexy," he spoke causing her to share his smile. He admired her standing there in a fitted pair of black jeans, a white button down blouse, and a simple black pair of Manolo's.

"Hey you," she spoke, so drunk in love with this nigga till she didn't know how she'd be able to let all of him go.

Zay pulled her in the doorway and started kissing her. She was lost for a moment in the deep kiss, but she pulled away from his grips, knowing that she was there on a mission. If she allowed herself to get caught up in his passion then she was going to be stuck between two men for the rest of her life and something had to give.

"Are you okay?" He asked, feeling a little tension in the air.

"We need to talk," she said, walking in past him. Zay followed her over to the sofa as she sat down.

"About what?" He asked with a concern look on his face, and then sat down beside her.

"About us," she started.

Zay just looked at her then decided to cut in. "I have something I'd like to share with you, too."

"Oh really?" Olivia said with a slight smile on her face as her eyes brightened. "You go first." She said, because in that moment if he wanted to fight for her then she was going to fight for him. Looking in his handsome face told her that he definitely had her heart and she could honestly see herself being with him.

"No, you go first." He insisted. He was ready to go all in, but he wanted to see if she was willing to go all in, too. If she was then it was over for Mark and he meant it.

She sat quiet for a moment, thinking about the earlier conversation with Mark. She loved her husband for the man that he was, but she wasn't in love with him and she definitely wasn't fully happy with him. She looked at Zay, because he had her heart, but would she be fucking up to leave a marriage that she'd invested so much in for someone that may not be who she was hoping he'd be?

Olivia's head began spinning for a moment as she tried to get the words out. "I love you. I've never been with a man that has shown me as much passion and desire as you've shown me. Its days when I wake up, feeling like I need you in my life and nights before I go to sleep, wishing that it was you laying next to me. I can't lie. I'm drunk in love with you." Zay smiled, because he liked where this conversation was going.

Olivia touched the back of his hand and continued. "I was so wrong for allowing this relationship to go as far as it has."

Zay's smile disappeared as his heart seemed to have stopped for a moment.

"I'm a married woman and I should act as such."

His eyes filled with water, but he held his composure as he stared at her.

"I'm so sorry," she said as her lips trembled, because it was breaking her heart just as much as his. She had to do it, though. Mark didn't deserve the things that she was doing to him. Plus, he called and wanted desperately to work on their marriage and downfalls. How could she deny him of that? "I'm so sorry," she said again. Those were the only three words she could get out at the moment, and then her eyes glanced down at the glass table in front of her as she saw the small, black jewelry box.

Zay's eyes followed hers to the box, and he quickly snatched it up.

Olivia tried wiping her eyes with the back of her hand. "Was that for me?" she asked with steady tears running down her face. "You weren't going to-"

"Nooooooo, how could I?" Zay quickly asked. "You're already married." He said, starting to feel played, used, and abused.

"I'm sorry," she said, feeling even worse now after seeing that small, black box. Her heart sank, wondering what was in it. Now, her thoughts drifted to what he wanted to talk about. How could she even ask him now? He looked hurt as she stared in his eyes. She could see the tears in his eyes, but not one tear fell as his facial expression began to harden a little.

"So, you came over here to completely break things off with me?" He asked, gripping the small, black box in the palm of his hand. He turned with a disappointed nod of his head. "So, you want to stay with a man that doesn't make you happy?"

"He wants to work on our marriage," she said, feeling so bad for hurting him.

"He wants to work on y'all's marriage?" Zay couldn't believe that she was willing to work on her marriage after she'd given him so much of herself in the past few months. "You gotta be kidding me?"

"I have to give him a chance." She cried. "I'd be less of wife not to."

"You're less of a wife now, standing in my face talking about you wanna make it work with your husband, but knowing you're in love with me." He attempted to walk off, but Olivia grabbed him by the arm.

"Please talk to me," she said. "Please."

"Please leave," he pushed her back off of him.

"I can't leave you like this."

Zay looked at her coldly. "Leave me like what? I'm good," he coolly said, but deep down he was beyond hurt. He was ready to fight over this woman. All she had to say was that she wanted him too and he would've.

"This conversation is over. This ridiculous meeting is over, because personally you could've called and told me this. You didn't have to come over."

"But, I wanted to see you." She cried.

"See me for what?" He asked, getting angry. "You wanted to see my cry?"

"Noooo," she said, shaking her head.

"You wanted to get some kind of reaction out of me, then?" But before she could answer, he kept talking. "You ain't going to see nothing, not even me no more. So leave," he demanded. Olivia could tell that he meant business and because she'd never seen this side of him before, she sadly turned and left.

Inside the elevator Olivia cried. It was a part of her that wanted to go back and apologize. If only she could jump in his arms and tell him that it would be alright and that she loved him so much. But that was so much easier said than done. She'd broken his heart and right now she knew it was nothing she could do to mend it.

She looked up at the floor display. 18…17…16…15… She reached out to maybe stop the elevator. Her heart was pounding. It was a feeling inside of her that told her once she'd left the building it was no coming back. Did she really want to leave the building and walk out of Zay's life for good?

9…8…7…6…

"Okay O', get it together," she told herself and quickly dried up her tears to the best of her ability. The elevator gradually came to a stop as it hit the first floor. Olivia stepped off while digging in her purse for her Gucci shades. No sooner than she could pull her shades out she bumped into Patricia.

"Oh heeeey, Olivia," Patricia spoke, completely caught off guard by seeing her.

"Hey," Olivia spoke, looking just as clueless as they stood there staring at each other.

"What you doing here?" they both asked at the same time, and then started smiling.

Olivia quickly put her shades over her eyes, knowing that she looked like she'd been crying. "Oh, I was just visiting with my realtor. Getting this building in Atlanta is proving harder than I thought." She faked a chuckle.

"Oh, I see." Patricia chuckled back, still unaware of what exactly was going on. "Well, I'm here to see my new man."

"You have a man?" Olivia pondered, not knowing anything about that. "That's great. Who's the lucky guy living in this building?" She asked, knowing that anybody that lived in that building had to have a little cake.

"His name is Xavier. I don't know if you saw him that day when he came in the salon. He was the one that the women were making a fuss over; because of the Bentley he drove."

Olivia's heart completely left her chest as she stood there looking like a fool. It was a good thing that the Gucci shades she was wearing, was covering the menacing look in her eyes. At that moment, she wanted to hurt Zay and Patricia.

"Oh, uh… I heard the fuss over him and I do believe that I remember who you're talking about. I only glanced him, though."

"Yeah, we've been talking to each other since that day. Girl, I think he's the one. With a dick that good, I ain't going nowhere."

Olivia cleared her throat. She was suffocating on her words just hearing that Zay had fucked Patricia. "You slept with him pretty quickly, huh?"

"Did you see him? Who in their right mind wouldn't? I'm claiming that hot sexy man. That's why I'm here now." She held up the bag in her hand. "I bought Chinese. That's what we ate the first time I visited."

Olivia pretended to be happy for her, even though she wanted to reach out and punch her in the throat. "Well, enjoy your lunch. I need to be making my way back to Augusta. My business is handled here." She said, brushing her hair down with her hand as a sign of feeling anxious.

"Okay we will, and be safe going back." Patricia said as she and Olivia went their separate ways. No sooner than Olivia could reach the lobby doors, she was calling Zay's phone.

"Hello," he answered, hoping that she was changing her mind.

"So, you're fucking my receptionist, Patricia?" She instantly asked with anger in her voice.

"What the hell are you talking about?" Zay quickly asked with a frown on his face.

"Just answer my question. Are you fucking Patricia?"

Zay was definitely caught off guard. He couldn't figure out how she would know that and obviously she'd just found out. "We had a one night stand back when your husband was suspecting you of cheating." He admitted.

Olivia shook her head, feeling more hurt than him now. "And to think I was going to leave my husband for you."

Hearing those words crushed Zay, because that's all he wanted her to ever do. He tried to get through to her. "I don't want that girl. She knows that."

"I can't tell, because she should be knocking on your door soon."

"No the fuck she shouldn't be," Zay said, starting to get angry.

"You're not who I thought you were." Olivia said.

Zay was even angrier now. "And you're not who the fuck I thought you were, either. And why should it matter who I've fucked, anyway? Aren't you still fucking your husband? Didn't you just break things off with me to work it out with him? Well, go do that." Zay said as he hung up in Olivia's face.

Olivia got to her car and hit the unlock button as she pulled the door handle and got inside it. She couldn't believe that things had turned out the way they had. God was certainly talking to her and she was listening. She sat inside the car for about ten minutes thinking, and then she picked up her phone to call her husband. He answered on the first ring.

"Hey love," she said.

"Hey baby," Mark spoke back. "What are you doing?"

"Nothing much," she said. "Just on my way to grab something to eat," she lied. "I just wanted you to know that I love you." She said. "We'll talk later."

"Okay baby," Mark said. "I love you, too."

"Okay," she said just above a whisper and with that, they ended their call. She'd told Mark that she wasn't going to come home until the next day, but she wanted to surprise him. Plus, she needed a good, long, sincere hug. She had fucked up in her marriage and she just wanted to make things right; not only with Mark but also with Felisha. She was her right hand and best friend and as soon as she and Mark ironed things out, she was going to pay her bestie a visit.

She headed down I-20 toward Augusta, GA. She was hurt, but glad that now she had some closure with Zay. He wasn't good for her, anyway. As she headed home, she called Zoe to let her know that she was going back a day early.

After speaking with Zoe for about five minutes, she then called Felisha, but she didn't answer. She decided to leave her a voicemail message.

Hey bestie. I just want things to be good with us. I hope you're doing okay and kiss lil Romeo for me. We have some catching up to do.

Chapter Eighteen

Felisha sat on the edge of her bed, feeling bitter. She hated that Olivia ended up with the life that she was supposed to have. Felisha's love for Olivia was twisted, because a part of her wanted Olivia to be happy. However, another part of her was torn between loving the person that had been there since pre-school or the man she'd fallen madly in love with eight years prior.

She looked over at Mark as he stood there not knowing what to say, because he knew that she was hurting. The look in her eyes was saddened, unlike the hopeful look he'd saw when they had gone to *The Master's* together a week prior. She stood up and walked over to him.

"You know that was her just calling me, right?"

"I know," he said. "She probably just wants to make sure that y'all are good."

"I don't know what to say to her right now." She said, strutting around him in a very sexy, satin baby doll nighty by Victoria Secret. "So, what'd she say when you spoke with her? Is she coming home?"

"Nah, she ain't coming home until tomorrow. She actually just called to check on me." Mark said, already feeling like he knew where this was going. He knew that what Felisha truly wanted she couldn't have and that would always interfere with her and Olivia's relationship.

"Don't you miss me, just a little bit?" She asked, circling him in slow motion, twirling in her hair.

"I thought you needed me to put the ceiling fan up in lil Romeo's room. How did we end up in here?" Mark asked shaking his head, and then nosily looking around. "What exactly did you need me to see in here?"

"I just needed you to see me," Felisha said, walking up on him and lightly kissing him on the lips. Mark quickly moved back.

"You know how I feel about my wife." He said, turning from Felisha and attempting to walk out her room. "This cannot happen."

Felisha grabbed him by the arm. "Don't leave. I miss you. I miss your touch. Don't act like you don't know what I can offer you. I know it's been four years, but you can't tell me that you've forgotten." She said, thinking back at the time she and Mark was last together. "We shared some special moment's together way before you even got married to Olivia. You remember, don't you?" She asked, breathing on his neck in hopes of seducing him.

"How can I forget it? I just don't care to think about it." He said, feeling hot all of sudden as he wiped the light specks of sweat off of his forehead. "It was a long time ago, Felisha. This thing initially started with our two month affair, some eight years ago. I told you that I was trying to figure out if I wanted to be in a relationship with the woman that I was with. Ironically, that person just so happen to be Olivia. I didn't know that you knew her. She never mentioned you to me nor did you ever mention her to me."

"Oh, here we go with that again," she cut in.

"You know I ain't lying." He said, tensely tapping his foot on the beige carpet.

"Yeah, but that's because we were both busy living our own lives. Plus, I didn't want to mention you if you weren't going to be with me. I was tired of telling O' about a boyfriend that she'd only get to meet once, because after that he was gone. I wanted to make sure that it was real between me and you, first."

"And I can understand that. However, Olivia never mentioned you to me, either. When we were together, it was about us and nobody else. All I know is that after I proposed to her, she wanted me to meet everybody. The first time I knew of your name and who you were, was the same day that she introduced us. Yes, I was probably more shocked than you, but I was honest with you by telling you that I was involved already. I just never spoke of with whom. I can't help that y'all didn't share things like who y'all was or wasn't fucking with. Being that y'all were best friends, I would think that you would've."

"And if we had, then what?"

"Then nothing," Mark said throwing up his hand. "That shit is behind us.

"Yeah, but when we met up that day, you could've said something after you saw that the best friend was me."

"Yeah, I could've," he spoke with sarcasm. "And, you could've said something, too. You should've called me out back then instead of sitting here looking sick about it eight years later."

Felisha dropped her head, because Mark was definitely telling the truth, but she still wasn't trying to hear it. "I could've, but I didn't. For the simple fact that you knew what she'd gone through after that situation with Sly. How could I say something? When she introduced you as her fiancé, what was I supposed to think, let alone say? When I'm sitting here being introduced to the nigga that I'd been fucking for the past two months," she said.

"I don't know, but this nonsense," Mark said, shaking his head. "This nonsense that you're pulling with O' gotta stop, as well as with me. You know how she feels about you and lil Romeo. She treats him like her own son."

"And I guess that should make me feel better?"

"Yeah, it should, because he still gets to spend a lot of time with me."

Felisha walked over by the window and stared out of it. Mark was lil Romeo's father and the man she loved more than anything, but she couldn't have him. Her best friend was relishing in the life that she was supposed to have.

Mark stood at the end of her bed. He couldn't leave her like this. She could very well be unpredictable and he couldn't afford any shit coming out about him and her or that kid.

"You can't keep up this crazy shit. What do you expect to gain by copping this attitude and talking shit about the past?"

"I can't help it. I'm finally getting my life together and all I can think about is if you were in it."

Mark shook his head. "You gotta get your mind right, Felisha. We hadn't slept together in four years. Hell, you've even been with more than a few nigga's since then."

"Yeah, but before that we used to sleep together all the time." Felisha said, almost sounding like she wanted the dick more than she wanted him.

"Come on," Mark said, like he was tired of her being in denial. He tried to keep his distance, but every blue moon he'd have to put her in check. Today was one of those days and he had to try to get through to her before she blew their cover. He walked over by her so he could look her directly in the face, and then he started.

"Look at me," he said as Felisha turned her head, already knowing where this was going. He gently grabbed her face and turned it toward him as he looked her directly in the eyes. "You already knew what time it was when we first started kicking it. True enough, I wasn't fucking anybody but you. However, I'd been seeing Olivia too and I liked her. That's why I told you what the deal was. She wasn't my woman, but I was getting to know her. Getting to know her, turned into me loving her, but in between all that--"

Felisha cut in. "You met me," she said, well aware of the story. She batted her sad eyes at him, feeling horrible about the situation. She walked over and sat on the edge of the bed. Being that close to Mark and not being able to have him was killing her softly.

Mark nodded his head, thinking back at that night some eight years prior. "You're right. I met you." He concurred. "I walked in the bar looking for a drink and I ain't gonna lie, probably some ass too. You were sitting there looking cute with that fat ass," he said, glancing down at her butt as it stuck out just a little under the short satin nighty she had on. "Shiiiit, I sat down right beside you."

Felisha smiled about that night which started off so innocent, and then ended up in an all night fuck session. She listened to Mark, because hearing about their first encounter always made her smile; especially if he was telling the story.

He continued.

"I started ordering drink after drink. I was horny and dealing with this fine ass lady that I wanted to make mine, but she wouldn't fuck nothing. We'd come so close that night, but it didn't happen." He said, now feeling somewhat comfortable enough to sit on the bed beside Felisha as he continued talking "You and I talked, you laughed, and I kept the drinks coming. Then the next thing I know, we're back at your place and we're going all in and I can't lie; I needed that more than you know." Felisha smiled inside, because she knew that he needed it too, in the way he sucked on her pussy and fucked her like she belonged solely to him. "From there we started fucking every other day, but I always told you that it was somebody else in the picture. Just because I never called her name, didn't mean that you didn't know."

"I never said that I didn't," Felisha slid in.

"I'm just saying, because once the shit was out in the open with me and Olivia; everything else started off as blackmail from you, which then turned into an arrangement that we kept a secret for two years." He said, having to remind her. "After you didn't tell Olivia that we had been seeing each other two months prior to her introducing us, I figured that you were cool with it. So, I continued to date her like you and I had never known each other. Then you're the one that called me out the blue, acting crazy." He said, now with feeling in his voice. "You were the one talking about if I didn't come over to your place that you were going to tell Olivia about us."

"That's because I was giving you time to come clean on your own. I was hurt when I saw the man that I was supposed to be introducing to my best friend show up to meet me, supposedly for the first time."

"Technically, you asked me if I'd go out with you for lunch and I told you that I might be able to. You know for yourself that I also said that depended on how long I would be with my girl. So don't act like you asked me to meet somebody, because you didn't." He said, causing Felisha to get a little agitated as she stood up in front of him. He tried his best not to admire her sexy, thick ass body as he continued. "You make it seem like I was supposed to show up with you when that wasn't the case at all Sometimes, I think you're delusional about this whole situation."

"Yeah, but if you would've showed with me then the cat would've been out the bag anyway."

"Could've, would've, should've," Mark mocked. "You could've ended this whole thing had you said something that day, but since you didn't back then; I don't understand why you would want too, now."

"Because I'm tired of pretending like I don't have feelings for you. I'm tired of pretending like we didn't exist."

"Felisha, you just wanna fuck. Let's just keep it real." Mark stated to Felisha's surprise as she stood there not saying a word. "You wanted this dick just like you do now. It's just that back then in order for me to keep my woman; you blackmailed me to get it. Hold up," he said, holding up his index finger. "Then when guilt had damn near choked me to death and I came to you feeling bad as hell about what we'd been doing, you came up with the arrangement. The arrangement was that as long as Olivia and I were engaged, you and I would still have sex since she wasn't giving up the goods until after marriage. I had my selfish reasons for agreeing to that, I'll admit it. God knows I would've gone insane waiting and I know that's no excuse, but that's just what it was." He said, thinking that two years was a long time without getting some pussy. "Then once we were married, that lil arrangement was supposed to be over."

"But, it wasn't, because we had sex again two years later." Felisha said, stepping up to him.

"Just once then, but that was different. I came to you, because I couldn't go to my wife."

"You couldn't go to your wife, because you knew she couldn't give you what I could."

"You might be right, because you gave me way more than I expected." He said as he thought back at lil Romeo and how aggressive Felisha could be in the bedroom and in getting what she wanted. He never thought she would've been so foolish to get pregnant on purpose, though. "If Olivia ever finds out about that, it would be over for the both of us." He reminded her.

"None of this would've started if you just would've told her," Felisha said.

"Why would I come clean with the woman that I chose to be with? If you weren't saying anything about it then I sure as hell wasn't saying anything, either."

"You should've just been a man about it and came clean." Felisha said, sounding like a scratched record. She wasn't even making any sense by this point.

"Whyyyyyyyy?" Mark dragged. "This shit been at least eight years ago. Why can't you let it go? I knew the situation was fucked up and I ain't gonna lie; I knew I loved you and the things you'd do for a nigga, but I loved her more." He said, knowing that Felisha was the sweet, round the way, down chick that would roll his blunts back when he smoked, but Olivia was the wholesome, business oriented, good girl that he could build a foundation with.

Felisha felt irritated and more than ever she just needed him to show her some kind of love or attention, but Mark was caught up in his feelings for his wife.

"I love her," he admitted, but he felt sorry for Felisha. She did deserve better, but she wouldn't allow herself to find it, because she was so drunk in love with him. He knew it and he also knew that if he ever left his wife that she would take him in and wouldn't give a fuck about her friendship with Olivia. He took sole blame for her behavior. He took advantage of an easy situation and for the entire two years of him and Olivia being engaged, he straight fucked Felisha senseless. It was no wonder she hadn't been broke a long time ago.

"You said that you'd always take care of us," Felisha said in hopes of getting through to him.

"I helped you get the nail shop didn't I?" Mark asked. "You know Olivia wouldn't have one hundred percent went in, had it not been for me pushing her to believe it was a good investment.

Felisha stood there for a moment. Mark wasn't lying about anything he'd said and she knew it. She also knew that she was the one drunk in love with him, not him with her. The truth was that she missed him like crazy, though. It had been years since he'd stuck his dick inside her, but for years she thought about it, she craved it, she wanted it and all she was waiting for was the perfect moment to get it.

"You don't even fuck her right. Don't you know she tells me this?"

"I have my reasons," he coolly said not wanting to turn Olivia out. "But, it ain't your business. I just want my wife to remain loyal to me and not get too far ahead of herself. She'll get all of me in due time."

"Keep on and somebody else is going to be getting all of her." She said, wanting so bad to tell him that Olivia was fucking another man since he kept her on a pedestal, but she kept quiet.

"She wouldn't do that."

"You never know what women will do these days when they ain't getting no action at home."

"You know something that I don't know?" He asked as his facial expression changed to nothing nice.

Felisha stood there for a moment, wanting to tell him everything, but instead she started unbuttoning his shirt.

Mark jumped up off of the bed. "What are you doing?"

"She can never love you like me and you know that she'll never fuck you like me." She desperately said and with that, she went back for the buttons on his shirt.

"Have you forgotten what happened the last time this happened?"

"Lil Romeo was conceived." She whispered, like that was nothing serious.

"And, that ain't happening no more," Mark said, pushing her away, but she pounced back on him.

"I know it ain't. I have a condom in the drawer if you want to use it. Plus, I'm taking birth control."

"I can't be fooling with you," Mark said, taking in a deep breath. Felisha smelled good, looked good, and almost had his dick rock hard. He could feel it growing down his thigh through his pants.

"You know she can never fuck you like me. Just admit it." She whispered in his ear, biting lightly on his ear lobe.

"Felisha stop," Mark said, knowing that Felisha was feisty and stayed horny. He also had begun to figure out that it was about that time for her to stir up some foolishness just so she could get the dick.

"You know you want it," she said, now bending on her knees and going inside his pants. "Please," she begged like a dog in heat. "Please, I just want to feel you inside me." Mark looked down at his shirt. She'd already taken all of his buttons loose except one. He backed away from her as she tried to get her hands in his pants. He headed for Felisha's bedroom door, but she was relentless in her pursuit.

"No," Mark said. "We made a vow that this would never happen again. You know that."

"The only thing I know is that I want you right now. It ain't like it has never happened, a hundred times over." She tried persuading him, now kissing around his neck and working her way to his chest as she massaged one nipple and succulently kissed on the other.

"I love my wife," he said, trying to deter Felisha.

She stopped kissing on his chest and looked at him side-eyed. "Who are you trying to convince?"

"I'm just saying." He tried backing away, but it was something about this that he missed. The thrill of it all had him horny and anxious. He struggled with his conscience as the lust of feeling her sweet kisses and her hands caressing his body, started taking over. For a moment, he thought he was still fighting her off, but in reality he was just standing there enjoying the warm feel of her mouth now wrapped around his dick.

"Let me give you what she can't." She whispered in between slurps.

"Shiiiit," Mark gave in with a moan, feeling her warm spit dripping between her fingers as she sucked and jacked him at the same time. This took him back as he thought about how he used to beat Felisha's pussy to death, just to relieve the pressure of not being able to fuck his fiancé.

"You like that?" Felisha asked in between sucking. This was all she wanted. She wanted to feel his thick cock in her mouth, because it made her feel special and good inside. Just having this moment could last her for a few more years of holding on to their secret.

"Suck it," Mark said, fucking the hell out of Felisha's mouth. "Suck it," he said again.

Felisha was doing just as she was told as she gave Mark some of the best head in the world. She was licking and slurping and jacking and popping, all the while playing in her pussy as her sweet juices dripped down her thighs.

"Mmm-mmm." She moaned; mouth full of dick.

"Eat that dick," Mark demanded. "Suck this big dick." He grabbed her head and shoved his dick in her mouth as far as it would go. "Eat it. Swallow it." Felisha was unnerved by his behavior, because that's how they always laid it down. Mark could be himself with her, whereas with Olivia, he treated her like she was the fragile one. "Take off that thing and bend over." He demanded.

Felisha happily came out of her baby doll satin nighty. Mark was also coming out of his clothes. The excitement of fucking her had taken over and even though he loved Olivia, he loved fucking Felisha more.

He stood back and watched Felisha's big, pretty round ass. She wasn't a skinny chick by far. She was definitely thick in the thighs with a wide, fat ass. She had a pudgy stomach and big breasts. Mark loved when they got together so he could ride her waves. She was sexy as hell to him and definitely cute in the face. If it wasn't for him choosing Olivia, it would've been her, hands down.

Mark walked over to her as she posed on the edge of the bed, doggy style. Her fat ass was up in the air with a deep arch in her back like she was begging for his attention.

"Come get it, baby." She said, pussy pulsating before he could even slide in it.

Mark walked over, opening up the nightstand drawer and grabbing a condom. He quickly tore open the pack and put it on. He wasn't taking any more chances like the time before. He then slid his dick up and down the crack of her ass. She moaned, anticipating the moment for him to go in deep. He then slapped her with his dick.

"You want this? Is this why you've been acting up?" He asked, now rubbing his dick up and down her wet pussy lips.

"Yes, I want it," she admitted. "Make me stop acting up." She begged.

"I knew you wanted it," Mark said and slid his dick in deep as she moaned with pleasure. Mark beat that pussy from the back, then the front, then the side. He even sat in a chair and let her ride him until her knees were shaking. He picked her thick, two hundred and three pound ass up in the air and fucked her standing up. Felisha was enjoying the dick down that he was giving her. Her pussy needed it just as bad as she wanted it.

An hour and two condoms later, Mark was now stroking his long rod inside Felisha's asshole. She took it any kind of way he gave it to her. Her ass was tight and warm as he was sliding his big pipe in and out of her with ease like he was fucking her pussy. It felt good to him as it gripped and pulled on his dick. He started to speed up, feeling a rush coming on.

"It's about to blow," he said, letting Felisha know what time it was. He stroked about a minute more then pulled his throbbing dick out as Felisha quickly turned around and started sucking it. In less than no time, Mark was shooting off loads of cum in her mouth. Felisha kept sucking, as she swallowed every bit of nut she could catch. "Aaaaaaaah," he said, feeling relieved. He hadn't gotten that buck wild in years, being that Felisha was the only woman he'd ever tipped out with on his wife.

No sooner than he could finish, he was already putting his clothes back on. "This can't happen again," he said.

"I know," Felisha responded with a smile on her face. She'd gotten what she wanted and now she was good.

Olivia was headed home, but had made a u-turn in hopes of mending her relationship with her bestie, first. She turned on Felisha's street and rode straight down to her house. She frowned upon pulling up in the driveway as she noticed Mark's car already parked there. She sat in the car for a moment, not really caring to think much of it. Maybe Felisha had called and needed something. Maybe he was there to speak with her about what had been going on between them. She didn't know why he could be there, but instead of getting out first, she sent Mark a text message.

What you doing? O'

He responded back quickly.

Missing you. Mark

Where are you, think I'm coming home? O'

I'm home. Come on, I'll cook us lunch so we can talk.

She quickly frowned. "Home?" She said, looking at the tail end of his car parked in front of her. "That's strange." She got out of the car and headed to the rear door. No sooner than she could bend the corner in the back yard, Mark was coming out the back door. He turned to look her right in the face. It was almost like he'd seen a ghost.

"What the fuck is going on here?" Olivia quickly asked as her voice nervously shook.

"Uh, hey Baby," Mark said while taking in a deep breath. Beads of sweat instantly popped off of his forehead. "I was just over here talking with Felisha about that lil situation you wanted me to handle."

"I thought you said that you were home just now in the text message."

"Well," Mark said, feeling tongue tied and caught up. "I wanted to surprise you since Felisha and I had talked, in hopes that things will now be good between y'all. I'm sorry about that. I should've been honest." Olivia didn't say a word as she heard Felisha's big mouth making its way to the back door.

"Heeeeeey babe," Felisha called out, trying to catch Mark before he left. "You're leaving your waaaaaatch." She dragged in shock, upon seeing Olivia standing in her back yard with her hands on her hips.

"Hey baby," Olivia said with a cut look in her eyes. "Hey baby," she repeated, looking from Felisha to Mark then back to Felisha. Her hands nervously shook some kind of bad as she tried to control herself.

"This ain't what it looks like," Felisha tried to clean it up as she ran her hands down her hair like anxiety had kicked in. Olivia looked over at Mark and then she peeped the buttons on his shirt were off by a button. Everything flashed before Olivia's eyes as she stood there almost speechless and hurt to the core at what she was witnessing.

How long had this been going on? Had it just happened for the first time? Who crossed the line first? A thousand questions flooded her mind in the few seconds she stood there.

"Baby," Mark called out. "Are you okay?" Olivia just stood there as the guilty look on Felisha's face told it all.

This nasty bitch just fucked my husband, she thought and before Mark could say another word, Olivia had gone mad.

"YOU DIRTY SON OF A BITCH!" She yelled out, slapping the spit out of Mark's mouth. "HOW COULD YOU DO THIS TO ME?!!!!" But, before he could answer, she was already trying to get to Felisha's ass. She had definitely blanked out and lost control of her emotions, but a bitch was going to tell her something and she wasn't leaving until they did.

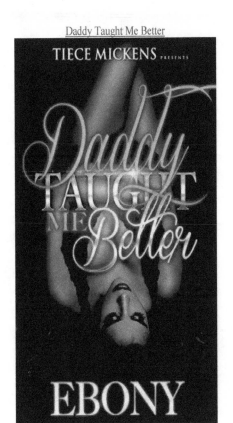

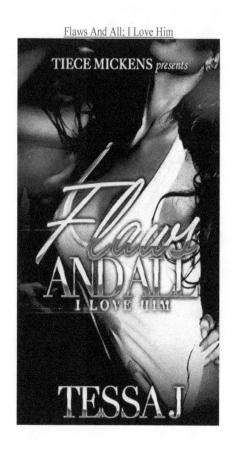

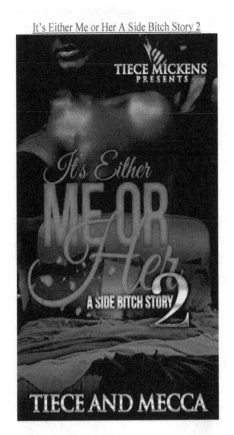

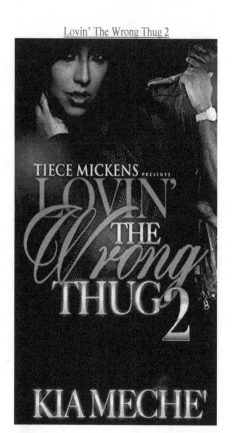